COPYCAT

C.S. BARNES

BLOODHOUND
— BOOKS —

Print ISBN 978-1-912986-41-5

To Pauline and Donald,
who knew that a detective novel would arrive one day

1

There was a thick fog rolling in across the playing fields. If it weren't for the distant sounds of barking and laughter, Sam could be forgiven for thinking she was there alone. It had been another sleepless night with Daisy, so to blow away the morning cobwebs on both mother and daughter, Sam had suggested that they walk Bonno together; Daisy had been delighted, of course. But with dog and daughter missing in action in the obscured landscape, Sam's bright idea suddenly seemed the exact opposite.

She swallowed down deep the growing ball of panic before shouting, 'Daisy, don't go too far now.' Sam paused, steadied the quiver. 'You don't want Mummy to lose you, baby, so come back a little okay.'

There was a giggle – 'You have to find us, Mummy.' – followed by a bark, as though the two had rehearsed their disappearing act to perfect their timings. 'You have to come into the fog and find us or–'

The break in Daisy's speech was abrupt; not the trail-away sound of a child distracted, but the snatch-away sound of something halting her mid-sentence, and Sam's panic swelled up through her chest again, settling in her throat, emerging in a 'Daisy!'

Sam's voice bounced around the empty field, echoing back to

her. She listened hard for the seconds that followed but she heard nothing; not Bonno's sniff or Daisy's voice, or even the shuffle of feet over frosted grass. Jesus, why had she dragged Daisy out here so early? Sam padded forward two steps at a time, pausing to listen to telltale signs around her between each shuffle.

'Daisy, baby, you're scaring me now.' Sam raised her voice, not to convey anger or annoyance but to try to carry her sound as far as she could across the field, reaching wherever her daughter was. When this last plea was met with more silence, Sam tried a different tactic. 'Bonno,' she sang, her voice softer; she followed the call with a gentle whistle. 'Bonno boy, where are you? Lemme hear you, boy.' Seconds later it came; a deep throaty bark, somewhere to her left. 'Good boy, Bonno, where are you?' Another bark came and Sam was away, her feet slamming into the hardened ground as she closed the gap between her and the still-barking dog.

It took longer than she expected – Bonno hadn't sounded that far from her – but eventually the fog gave way to the sight of her daughter, kneeling with her back towards Sam, with Bonno a further two feet in front of Daisy.

Sam bent over, her hands pressed flat against her knees while she panted air into her chest. Her daughter didn't move, as though oblivious to Sam's arrival. Meanwhile Bonno carried on barking, and it wasn't until Sam glanced up that she realised he hadn't been barking for her at all, but at something near him, in front of him. She took two hesitant steps toward her daughter, setting a hand flat on the girl's shoulder to pull her attention round. Daisy's face was twisted with confusion, and behind her, Sam saw the silhouette of someone lying flat on the ground, Bonno barking just beyond them.

'Mummy, why would the lady sleep here?'

Something in Sam snapped and she flew into action. In a single movement, she scooped up her daughter, angling her away from the body laid out in front of them both. She clicked her fingers once, twice, until Bonno's barking gave way and he was sitting upright at her side – he, like Sam, couldn't take his eyes off the body. A woman, fully clothed but frozen by the harshness of the previous night's weather, her body set at the wrong angles as though she had frozen mid panic, mid struggle.

'Why aren't we waking her up?' Daisy asked, her question pressed into her mother's shoulder. 'Why aren't we taking her home?'

Sam shushed her daughter and bopped gently up and down, as though Daisy had transformed into an infant in these minutes. As Sam started walking, she pressed a hand against the back of her daughter's small head. 'We'll tell someone, baby, we'll get to the edge of the field, where the lights are, and we'll tell someone, and they'll take her home. Does that sound okay?'

Daisy nodded and Sam exhaled quietly, forcing out tension, panic, feelings that she couldn't quite identify due to their unfamiliarity. She padded back in the direction that they'd come from, the ground already softening underfoot as the frost gave way to the growing temperature, but Sam felt a chill all over.

At the edge of the park, she set her daughter down on a sturdy wooden bench, clipped Bonno's lead back to his collar, and pulled her phone out from the inside pocket of her coat.

'Hello,' she stuttered, her teeth chattering down the line to the operator. 'Hello, I'm at Woodfield playing fields, with my daughter, and our dog, and we've just found someone here who needs help, I think.' Sam ran two fingertips along her forehead, inhaled deeply to steady herself. The operator was midway through her follow-up question when Sam started again, speaking over her: 'We've found a woman,' she managed. 'A body.'

2

By the time the alarm went off, DI Melanie Watton had already been awake for nearly ten minutes. She counted the seconds in time with her clock, determined for once not to get out of bed and get ready for work any earlier than she needed to. The words of her mother rang around her head for each of those waking moments though: 'You're married to your work, Mel.' The alarm tone ended up being a welcome interlude.

She hit the snooze button, sat upright in bed, and thumbed through her phone's list of most used apps until she found the Radio Local logo. She flicked on the phone's Bluetooth to connect it to the speaker set on her dressing table and waited for the host's voice to fill the room – 'Goooood morning, folks, we're bringing you the best of the best on Radio Local this morning. Coming up later we've got...' – before she padded toward the bathroom. Melanie had grown to like the sound of someone else's voice in the mornings. She showered, dressed, didn't make the bed, and she took herself from bedroom to kitchen to make something that resembled breakfast.

Melanie was two sips into her coffee when the radio was cut through with the sound of her phone ringing. The screen displayed

DS Edd Carter's work number and, before 8:00am, Melanie knew that he couldn't be calling with good news.

Edd closed the door to the bathroom, inhaled deeply, and hit Dial on his boss's work number. She had answered after three rings, her voice already sharp, concerned. 'What?'

'Boss, it's me. I've just had a call from dispatch, some woman and her daughter have found–'

'Daaaaaaaaddy.' Emily's voice drifted in from outside the bathroom door.

Edd placed a hand over the speaker. 'Two seconds, sweetheart, Daddy's on the phone.' Uncovering the speaker, he started afresh. 'They've found a body, a woman, that's about as much as I know. Uniforms went to the scene to verify things and apparently they've had–'

'Daddy, this is a really long wee,' came the same childish voice from before.

Edd's embarrassment was overshadowed by concern. 'What is, Emily, mine or yours?' He was plagued by images of a house covered in Christ only knows what. From outside the door, he heard a giggle that unnerved him.

'Yours, Daddy, I'm not on the toilet, so I can't be weeing.'

Edd breathed a heavy sigh. At least he'd taught his daughter something.

'Carter?' His boss's voice pulled him back into their conversation.

'Sorry.' He rubbed at his forehead. In one great and almighty pull at his insides, he realised how much he missed his wife. 'Trish is away for an evening and I'm not big on Daddy Day Care, you see,' he offered, to explain the morning madness, but Melanie gave him no reply. 'Where had I got to?'

'Uniforms. A fright.'

He nodded. 'They've had quite a fright, yes, something about the woman looking like – Jesus!' The bathroom door burst open and in came Emily, with a messy circle of butter on each cheek. 'Emily, what are you doing?' His daughter skipped around him, a wide smile on her face that made the greasy circles look all the more out of place. 'Boss, I've got to go.'

He disconnected the call and dropped his phone back into his pocket, scooped up his daughter and carried her back into the kitchen. 'I left you having breakfast,' he said, assessing the damage while Emily made herself comfortable on a breakfast-bar stool. Edd pulled partially chewed toast from the sink and replaced it with Emily's empty plate; it was impossible to discern how much his daughter had eaten, and how much she'd hidden around the kitchen for a delayed discovery later in the day – although her frantic giggles made the idea of hidden breakfast foods seem like an absolute certainty.

Edd inhaled hard and exhaled through his mouth, forming a perfect O to force the air out. It wasn't her fault; kids will be kids.

'When's Mummy coming home?'

But he lost his composure then. Edd's shoulders hunched as though a cry was inevitable but he tried, like he'd tried every morning for the last week and a half, to stifle an outburst. 'She's just away for another night, Em,' he said, not turning to face his daughter; quietly praying that she wouldn't catch him in a lie.

'That can't be right.' Edd heard his daughter hop from the stool and land on the kitchen floor with a soft thud. 'She said she was only going away for a night and it's been loads of nights. Have you asked?' She was tugging at the loose edge of his unironed shirt, pushing for his attention. 'Have you tried asking her, Daddy, when she's coming back?'

'No, I haven't. I haven't tried asking.' He wasn't quite ready to admit out loud just how scared he was of what his wife's answer might be.

. . .

DC Chris Burton was pulling her hair into a tight ponytail when her phone rang.

'Boss?' she answered, one hand holding the half-complete hairdo in place.

'How soon can you be at the playing fields?' Melanie's curtness matched the DC's. They each held a deep respect for the no-nonsense conduct of the other. Economical with their words and quick with their decision-making, Chris had been an obvious choice when Melanie was tasked with putting together an incident team three years earlier.

Chris threw a quick look at the bedroom clock before answering.

'I can be ready in ten minutes,' she said.

'I'll meet you there,' Melanie replied and disconnected the call.

Chris had learnt not take any offence. She finished pulling her hair into place, grabbed her black cardigan from the back of the chair next to her, and made her way out while tugging the garment on.

She was halfway down the stairs when she heard the kettle whistle to a boil, but she didn't have time for tea, or the accompanying, 'Morning, love,' small talk that Joe would expect with it. Chris took the last few steps slower, hoping to disguise the sound of her coming down them at all, but as she rounded the corner towards the coat stand there Joe was, a steaming cup of tea held out toward her.

'There's toast too,' he said, flashing a smile.

Chris shook her head and reached past to the coats hanging behind Joe. She grabbed a light brown mac and as she pulled on the extra layer, explained, 'I've got to get to work.'

Joe looked down at his watch. 'You're not on the clock yet.'

'We're the police, Joe.' She took the tea from him and swallowed a large sip. 'We're always on the clock.'

Chris picked up her satchel from behind the front door and lugged it over her shoulder. She made a show of taking another sip of tea before handing the mug back to her husband.

'Toast?' he tried.

'I'll grab something in the canteen,' Chris answered, but Joe wore a disbelieving expression. 'I promise,' she lied. She left an abrupt kiss on her husband's cheek before heading for the front door, her thoughts already tied up with what might be waiting for her.

3

DI Melanie Watton stepped over the police-tape cordon that surrounded the playing fields. The PCs in charge of manning the barrier batted back the crowds that tried to follow her through. There was a medley of photographers and reporters bound up with bloodthirsty civilians. Whatever their motivations, everyone was trying to get a good look at the scene of crime officers, the police constables, the arriving detectives. It was always the same, Melanie thought; where there was tragedy, there were happy onlookers.

She tried to drive out her distaste for the madding crowd as she walked closer to the incident tent, erected, Melanie assumed, over the body that was being examined. She cast a look around the surroundings – grey skies and muddied grounds from days upon days of rain – and she had to admire the determination to keep the crime scene clean, although it seemed likely that irreparable damage had already been done. As she approached the final cordon – a smaller, closer circle of trust that existed around the immediate crime scene – she was given overalls and shoe covers. From the corner of her vision, she spotted DC Chris Burton, manipulating herself into the same attire that Melanie had just been given.

'I didn't realise you were here already,' Melanie said, leaning down to hook a plastic casing around her black boot.

'I rushed. Early bird and all that.' Chris sounded jovial as she zipped together her torso's white plastic covering. She had always hated this gear. At her first crime scene, Chris had joked that the overalls made her feel like she was tucking herself into a body bag. It had been met with laughter by the team at the time, but she'd never quite escaped the feeling. She smoothed down the front of her suit and glanced at her boss who was zipping up her own protective gear.

The two officers made their way towards the small tent, housing the woman that had brought them all here. There was a hive of activity to pass through on their way though. Overalls continued to scour the surrounding areas, scraping samples from different parts of the playing fields, collecting whatever maybe-evidence they could find.

'I've got something!' one voice shouted and while Chris's attention was pulled to the SOCO in question, Melanie stayed her course, pushing through the loose flaps of the evidence tent and arriving at the foot of a young woman – her skin mottled, her clothing muddied, and her life quite clearly extinguished.

'I didn't think anything in the world could get you away from that lab,' Melanie said, crouching down to the hooded figure sitting cross-legged on the wet ground. 'To what do we owe this honour?'

George Waller pulled down his medical mask revealing a pale face that was trying, but failing, to force a smile.

'Truthfully, I wish I hadn't bothered.' Hands flat on the floor, he levered himself into a standing position and assessed the body splayed out before them both. 'Suffocation, I'd guess, hence the bag.' He pointed to the clear wrapping, still secured around the woman's neck. 'She struggled, hence the state of all this.' He pointed to her parted legs, her widespread arms.

George shook his head. 'I'll know more when we've got her back at the lab, obviously, but cause of death is fairly clear. Time of death will be difficult, due to,' he faltered, waved an arm beyond the tent as though gesturing to the general state of the world rather than the October weather. 'As I said, we won't know the fine details until we've had a proper look, and we won't have a proper look until...' he trailed off again. It looked as though something was troubling him but without more information, Melanie couldn't guess at what.

'What's so bad about this one, George?' Melanie knew how she sounded, but she didn't have the patience to soften herself with a trying case already laid in front of her.

'A couple of things, really.' George crouched down to his open kit case. 'Firstly, there's this.' He handed Melanie a clear evidence bag that contained a square of paper, no bigger than a few inches, on which was a handwritten message: *Remember me?*

'When we rolled her over, looking for any other obvious injuries or obstructions before we moved her...' George paused, removed his glasses to deliver a firm rub at each eye, and started again. 'We found that tacked to her back. Like a playground bully, you know?' He almost laughed. 'Like a kick me sign.'

Melanie held the note up to the light outside the tent to continue her inspection. 'Okay. Help me out here, George, you said there were a couple of things.'

He replaced his glasses. 'That's the thing, you see. The place,' he gestured again somewhere beyond the tent, 'the body, the method.' He pointed to the woman on the ground and seemed to lose himself in thought for a second before he concluded, 'I do remember all of this. I've seen this murder, in this place, before.'

DS Edd Carter pushed the door gently, hoping to slip into the office without drawing too much attention to himself. As the door clicked shut, just as quietly as it had opened, Carter shot a cautious look around the room. He was met with half-empty desks, and those that were occupied had distracted officers sitting at them, far too preoccupied with their work to notice a latecomer. When Carter glanced in the direction of his DI's office, he let out a heavy sigh on seeing her door was shut and her view of the outside space obscured.

'Don't feel too relieved,' a voice from behind him announced. 'She already knows that you weren't on time this morning, there's no getting around it.'

DC Chris Burton had slipped through the door behind her colleague while he had assessed the room. She stepped around him, heading toward her own desk that was just outside of their senior's own space. 'Where were you, mate?' Her tone had been accusatory to begin with, but the mate softened it.

Carter sighed. 'Emily, she's... time-consuming, especially first thing in a morning.' He moved toward his desk as he spoke, pulled out his chair, and landed heavily on the seat of it. 'It took forever to get her up, dressed, to find all the toast.' Chris moved to interrupt him, but Carter undercut her. 'It's best you don't ask.'

'Trish not around this week?' Edd's face changed and Chris spotted it. 'Sore point?'

'It's best you don't ask.' He repeated, swinging round to face his computer screen which was slowly spinning into life. 'Want to fill me in on what I missed this morning?'

Chris turned to face her own computer. 'Body, park, woman.' A series of mouse clicks followed. 'Plus, a slew of headlines.' She angled her screen for Edd to see news article after news article announcing the death of a young woman in the local area. 'She was found by a woman out with her dog and her daughter. She didn't seem especially eager to talk to us, so I doubt she'll talk to the press, but no doubt that'll spur the fuckers on.' Chris pulled her screen back around. 'Anyway, there was no ID, so here we are.' She gestured to the determined officers dotted around the room. 'Playing "Guess Who" with our victim for the time being.'

The main door to their office banged open clumsily and in wobbled a young PC, fresh-faced and balancing a packed evidence box between both arms. No one moved to help him, but within seconds of his noisy entrance, Melanie yanked her office door open and scanned the room for the source of the noise. She nodded at the young officer.

'Michael Richards?' she asked.

'No, ma'am. PC Shields. I was asked to–'

Melanie lifted the evidence box from the young man, making it look half the weight that his stagger had implied it was. Setting it down on the nearest desk, she twisted the box from one side to another until she found what she was looking for: *Michael Richards* written along one bottom edge of the box in black marker. The young PC laughed.

'Oh, I thought–'

'Thanks, chap, you've done a good job there.' This time it was Chris's turn to interrupt the young man; if for no other reason than to protect him from the embarrassment that Melanie would no doubt inflict, had he kept on with his rambling. It wasn't anything personal; it was just the mood that murder tended to put the boss in. 'Anything else for us?'

PC Shields faltered. 'Ah, should there be?'

'This is everything, thanks,' Melanie said, already pacing back to her office.

Edd gave the youngster an apologetic smile before pushing himself away from his desk. Despite her wrath, Edd followed Melanie into her room where she was unpacking the contents of the box she'd just been given. Chris joined him in the doorway in time to hear Melanie's response to whatever Edd's query had been.

The DI eyed an old mugshot as she spoke. 'Apparently, he's the one who committed this murder the first time around.'

4

Backsides were on seats and eyes were glued to the whiteboard at the front of the room, decorated with the faces of five young women, tacked together in one corner of the large space. Alongside these five women there was a police mugshot of an older man. In block capitals, DI Melanie Watton wrote MICHAEL RICHARDS next to the man's face before setting the board marker down and turning to address her team. DS Carter and DC Burton were at the front of the room, as usual, and behind them there sat an additional six officers, poised and ready for whatever their superior knew.

'Is Michael Richards a familiar name to anyone in this room?' Melanie asked, and with notable hesitation, DC Lucy Morris put her hand up. 'Morris,' Melanie called her out. 'What do you know?'

'He murdered five women, about twenty years ago, around these parts,' she said, her voice fragmented and nervous. 'Five women in five months, and after the fifth one, he turned himself in.' She paused, hoping that this would be explanation enough, but Melanie urged her to continue. 'He said five was enough to make him famous.' A disgruntled moan travelled around the room with no specific source, and Melanie nodded her agreement.

'It didn't make local news all that much because frankly he's someone we'd rather forget.' Melanie took back the baton of addressing the room. 'But six months ago, Richards was murdered in prison.'

'Shame.' DC David Read piped up from the back of the room and Melanie couldn't help but smirk. She agreed, whole-heartedly, but knew it wouldn't be proper to admit out loud in front of a room of colleagues, so instead she ignored the remark and continued.

'Looks as though he ended up two cells down from a relative of victim number three, Penny Evans.' Melanie pointed to the board as she spoke. 'Penny's older brother was in for drug use, stabbed Richards in the shower, and there ends that story.' Another groan rumbled up from her audience. 'The start of another story though, seems to be this,' she said, turning to tack another picture to the board. Above the image she wrote, *Donna Clements, 1998*. The image itself showed a young woman lying on a patch of grass, her limbs kicked out at wild angles, a clear bag round her head and fixed down with blue tape at her neck. Alongside this image, Melanie pinned another: the young woman from the park, bag still around her head, lifeless limbs stretched out on the grass around her. Above this second image, she wrote *Jane Doe, 2018*.

'Jesus,' Read erupted again. 'They could have been staged.'

'Maybe they were,' Carter added.

Melanie remained quiet while the team advanced their discussion and she tacked two more pieces of evidence to the board. One, she pinned alongside the image of Donna Clements, and this additional picture showed a handwritten note adorned with the message: *Me again.* When this was fixed in place, she added an image of the note that had been left beneath their new victim: *Remember me?*

'Richards didn't leave a note on his first victim, but Donna, his second victim, was the start of this trend.' Melanie read from an open folder to pass on these details of Richards' original crimes. 'After her, he left a note on all of them, including the final victim whose note read *Catch me if you can.*'

'Tosser.' It was Burton this time, and Melanie shot her a disapproving look. 'I'm not taking it back,' the DC added, and Melanie let the comment go. Again, it was hard to criticise something she agreed with.

Melanie threw the folder down on the desk closest to her. 'He was caught, he was arrested, and he was convicted. His family moved out of the area, and that was the end of it.'

'What about the families of the victims?' Read piped up.

'What about them? They're unlikely to try to frame a dead man for a murder, Dave,' Chris chimed in before her boss could.

'Chris has got a point,' Melanie added. 'The victims' families are a mixed bag anyway, some are still local, some moved away but still have ties to the area. Either way, depending on how far this goes, talking to those families might be a possibility in the near future.'

'Great,' Edd grumbled, his eyes upturned.

'Nice lie-in this morning?' Melanie asked pointedly but picked up her speech before he could defend himself. 'The priority for now though is working out who this victim is.' She paused to pin a final picture to the board behind her. It was the same woman from the earlier 2018 victim shot, but this photograph was taken at a slightly different angle; her face, still sheathed in muddy plastic, was more visible, more stricken, and younger than Melanie would have guessed from the girl's clothing.

The team eyed the image quietly for a second and Melanie allowed a deliberate amount of time to pass, long enough for the image to stick with her team, long enough for it to drive them.

'Where are we on an ID? I'll ask the obvious question,' DC Brian Fairer asked, breaking his silence on the incident so far. 'Do we have missing persons to check through, recent reports, what?'

'Morris?' Melanie deferred the question to her startled DC.

Lucy straightened her back before answering; she was visibly tense. 'I've been talking to some of the PCs, and I've had a look at the latest logs. The most recent report actually came in first thing this morning.' She paused to adjust her glasses, reading details from the notebook in front of her. 'Local couple, Robert and Evie Grantham.' She intoned their names as though asking a question but when the young DC looked up from her notes, she found five sets of eyes staring back blankly. 'Of course, they called first thing to say their daughter didn't come home last night, but didn't say she was staying at a friend's either, and she hasn't...' Morris trailed off, fidgeted in her seat and adjusted her glasses again.

'Go on,' Melanie encouraged her. 'There's more.'

Morris swallowed hard. 'Their daughter is called Jennifer, but known as Jenni, and she's currently studying for her A Levels at Woodfield College.'

'Fuck.'

Melanie heard the expletive but couldn't isolate the source. 'That makes her how old?'

Morris hesitated. 'She's turning seventeen next month.'

'There's no way that body is sixteen,' Read called out but despite his forced confidence, even he didn't sound convinced. 'She's dressed older, isn't she? She could be into her thirties from those clothes, I'd guess.' He looked around at his colleagues for support, but nothing came. From their own viewpoints, they all stared at the image tacked to the incident board. 'Is anyone looking at that and seeing a sixteen-year-old?'

'Jesus Christ, Read, if you can't tell a sixteen-year-old from a grown woman that's your bad shout,' Carter finally cracked, craning around in his seat to stare down his opposing DC.

'Lads,' Melanie started. 'Try to stay–'

The door swinging open at the back of the room cut through her intervention. The same yuppy PC as before – Melanie felt around for his name but couldn't find it – stood holding what looked to be a photograph. His eyes skated over the superior officers seated before him but settled on the spread of bodies pinned to the imposing whiteboard.

'I was asked to bring this,' he said, to no one in particular, eyes firmly in place.

'And what is this?' Melanie said, closing the gap between them. She took the photograph from him and stared down at the image of a young girl, wearing a pale green T-shirt and a Woodfield College waterproof which she had draped over her legs. Denim jeans and brilliant white converse poked out from beneath the overall. She was smiling, and beautiful, and definitely no older than sixteen. Melanie let out a heavy sigh. 'Where did you get this?'

'A man came in and left it at reception, said something about his daughter being missing.' PC Shields shook his head, as though physically pulling his attention away from the image display. He addressed Melanie directly. 'Sorry, he said that his daughter was missing, and he'd spoken to someone earlier this morning who had asked for a picture.' Melanie didn't answer the question, merely nodded in encouragement. 'He thought it would speed things up, he said, if he could bring it straight down and leave it with someone. Desk Sergeant said it might be of interest to you up here.'

'Desk Sergeant was right.' Melanie fixed her eyes on the shot of the girl again, but the young PC coughed, pulling back her attention. 'If that's all, PC, you're free to head out. Thanks for bringing this up to us.' She turned to walk back to her post at the front of the room.

'Is it her?' the young officer asked and when the DI turned to face him, he asked again, 'Is it the girl from the park, do you think?'

'Too soon to say,' Melanie answered, holding eye contact with him. 'Thanks again.' This time when she turned to walk away, the young officer took his cue to leave.

'Too soon to say?' Burton pushed when Melanie resumed her standpoint.

The DI turned to pin the picture to the board. 'We're going to need a Family Liaison.'

5

DI Melanie Watton knew the local streets well enough to navigate her way to the Granthams' house without needing any GPS guidance. She drove silently with DS Edd Carter in the passenger seat. In her peripheral vision, Melanie could see her junior throwing the occasional look her way. They were still five or so minutes away from the property when Carter said, 'Penny for your thoughts?' Melanie knew she'd been quiet with him all morning. It was part-frustration, she had to admit – the repeated late arrivals weren't a good sign – but she also knew her DS likely had good reasons for them. But her silence also came from a second source of frustration.

Melanie sighed. 'This is just the shit part, isn't it,' she said without breaking her gaze on the streets that flowed past them.

'I can take lead?' Carter offered.

'I'm the SIO on this.'

'I know, but–'

'I'm the SIO,' Watton said again, silencing her colleague.

Melanie wasn't territorial, although she'd been accused of it once or twice. But she didn't like implicit suggestions that the job was too much, too hard for her. It was too hard for everyone sometimes, and on her way to this post she'd seen more than one senior officer go to pieces over a case, but this wouldn't be the one that broke her – she'd already decided. She was too young, too new to this, to be broken so early.

In the brown cardboard wallet that lay across her lap, there was a close-up image of the victim's face, the steel of George Waller's examination table visible behind her head. This would be difficult, Melanie knew, but she would be fine; she had to be.

They arrived outside of the house to find Robert Grantham standing on the doorstep already; they had called ahead to warn the couple of their arrival and Mr Grantham looked braced, ready for whatever might be coming. As the pair unclicked themselves from their safety belts and seats, another car pulled in behind them. Carter clocked the vehicle in the rear-view mirror and shot his boss a look.

'I asked DC Dixon to come along, just in case,' Melanie explained without meeting her colleague's face. DC Ian Dixon was one of the best Family Liaison Officers the team had worked with, and there was meaning to take away from Melanie having asked him to assist with this case. Melanie knew what was about to unfold, and both her and Carter were ready for it. 'He'll wait outside while we make early contact and we'll go from there,' she explained, stepping out of the car and closing the door before Edd could proffer a response. Carter followed her, locked the vehicle behind him, and caught up with his boss in three easy strides along the driveway to the house.

'Mr Grantham, I'm DI Melanie Watton and this is my colleague DS Edd Carter.' Edd nodded a subdued hello but Robert Grantham didn't seem to notice. 'Thank you for making time to see us today. We understand you're very distressed and eager for some answers. Might we come in?'

The father looked momentarily confused; he shook his head lightly, as though shaking something away, and then he stepped to one side. 'Of course, of course,' he said, more to himself than the officers. 'Come in, please. My wife, Evie, she's in the living room.' The officers lingered just inside the hallway. 'Oh, the living room is down there on the left, the first door.' The officers followed the instructions and seconds later the four individuals were united inside an exceptionally neat living area.

The walls were a neutral off-white, the floors were a dark wood, and the furniture looked as though it had been lifted from a Victorian catalogue – but something about the room seemed to suit the appearances of the Granthams entirely. Robert Grantham, an older man than Melanie had been expecting, was dressed in tailored trousers that were carefully creased down each seam and a pale green button-down shirt. Small bags were appearing beneath his eyes and his hair was dishevelled, as though fingers had been run through it recently.

Meanwhile, Evie Grantham was picture perfect in her attire but less so elsewhere; where her husband's eyes were heavy, Evie's were bloodshot. The red cloud that sat around each eye was a telltale sign of the tears that had been shed over the morning, and Melanie felt it in her gut that there were only more to come.

Both officers introduced themselves again to Evie Grantham. The woman gestured for them to sit down on the sofa opposite her own, and Melanie noted how neither of the seats were angled towards the television. They must entertain a lot, she thought, although she wasn't sure whether this said more about the Granthams or herself.

'Mr Grantham—' Melanie started but the man held a hand out to interrupt her.

'Robert,' he said, his hand flat against his chest. 'Evie.' He gestured to his wife.

'Robert,' Melanie revised her opening. 'Might we ask one or two questions about your daughter? Her usual haunts, behaviours.' Robert nodded Melanie to continue. 'You told dispatch that it wasn't like her to be out all evening. Was there anything happening last night that you were aware of; a social gathering of any kind?'

Robert hesitated, so his wife stepped in to answer. 'She was with friends, we knew that much,' she said, but paused to take a deep breath as though steadying herself. 'There wasn't a party or anything, not that we were told about, and Jenni would have always told us. They were all very excited about Halloween, you know how they get; it only seems to get worse as they get older. She was at a friend's house and she said she'd be late because they were going to test out their costumes, a trial run or something. So we knew she'd be late, but that wasn't a concern, really, it's never been...' She trailed off, her shoulders hunching up as she gave way to a deep sob. 'I'm sorry, I'm so sorry, I just, I don't understand how this, how this is happening.'

Robert rested a hand on his wife's leg and leaned in to kiss the side of her temple. 'Jenni is a young woman and we've trusted her to come back at a decent time. Even when she says late, she doesn't really mean late, it's just that we go to bed early ourselves.'

'Do you usually hear Jenni come home?' Melanie asked.

'No.' Robert was firm in his response, as though he had anticipated this type of question. 'My wife has problems with her health, her medication usually wipes her out come half past nine, and I'm of the sleeping tablet generation, I'm afraid, so we're both fairly useless after around ten in the evening. Which is why we never overmonitored Jenni's times.' He sounded defensive, which was quite natural, given the circumstances. Parenting skills were usually called into question on cases like these.

'Do you know which friends Jenni was with last night?' Carter intervened.

Robert looked to his wife for an answer. 'Yes, yes, she was with Eleanor Gregory. Her house is about a ten-minute walk from here, but they might have been going to meet others. Jen, she'd got quite close to Elanor and a few others since their A Levels started.' Evie paused while Carter made a note of this. 'Eleanor seems like a nice girl, from the few times that we've met her.'

'Do you know anyone else who's likely to have been with them?' Melanie added, allowing her colleague time to finish his scribing.

Evie Grantham shrugged. 'There could have been any number of them, I suppose. There's a chap, Peter, Paul, P-something. He's usually at Eleanor's heels, so I suspect he will have been there. Other than that, it will have been the girls from their year. Oh God, what's his name? P–'

'Patrick?' her husband interrupted her.

'Patrick, yes!'

Melanie shot a side glance at her junior to make sure that he was getting the details down as the couple spoke. Edd underlined the name Patrick three times and then nodded to his boss to continue with her questions. The DI took a deep inhale as she opened the brown folder that lay flat across her lap; this was going to hurt.

'Mr and Mrs Grantham,' she said. She needed the formality, the safe distance, before she could get to this next part. 'You may or may not have heard that we found the body of a young woman over on the playing fields early this morning.'

Evie Grantham's hand shot up to her mouth to cover her pursed lips, as though she were physically holding in an outburst; she looked away from Melanie, but the woman's husband encouraged the officer to continue. 'There was no form of ID on the body, but we asked the Medical Examiner's office to supply us with a photograph.' The image was out of the folder, firm in Melanie's hand but still facing her torso, concealed from the couple. 'I can't imagine how troubling this must be for you both, really, but if you could look at this picture and confirm for us whether it is or isn't Jenni, we'd be a step further in finding out what's happened here.'

Robert Grantham closed the small gap between him and his wife, wrapping an arm tight around her shoulders. He kissed the side of her temple again and nodded his approval for Melanie to continue. The DI handed the picture over with a watchful eye on the couple, waiting for their primary reactions. As she watched Evie Grantham crumple into her husband like a paper doll, Melanie knew that the morning's victim was indeed the sixteen-year-old Jenni Grantham who had gone missing some time during the night – and she knew too, that this family was changed forever.

Melanie gave Edd the signal to bring in Dixon from his standpoint outside, so Carter excused himself while the bereaved parents shared a quiet moment. It was uncomfortable for Melanie to be so close to their grief, but she could at least avert her eyes, instead choosing to scan the room for sights and sounds of their victim. Jenni was everywhere; there were photographs at every age, family portraits and birthday parties surrounded by friends. It would be clear to anyone who stepped into this space that the Granthams were a couple who doted on their daughter, and this news had carved a hole that would take some time to repair – assuming it could ever be done. Melanie had seen families torn apart by death before, but it was too soon, too fresh to say whether this would be another of those times.

'Did she suffer, Miss Watton?' Robert asked, his wife still hunched into him. Her tears had bated but her eyes were fixed open, staring intently at a spot on the carpet. She didn't acknowledge that her husband had spoken, nor did she acknowledge Melanie's answer.

'I'm afraid that we're not yet sure of the incidents surrounding Jenni's death, Mr Grantham.' Melanie wanted to lie but her deeprooted professionalism wouldn't allow for it. 'The Medical Examiner has assured me that this case is at the top of his list though, so we should know more in the next day or so.' Robert Grantham nodded absently, as though he might not have fully heard, or understood, the DI's response. 'It's very early days,' she added. 'But there's no reason at all to think that we won't catch the person responsible for this.'

Evie Grantham snapped back into the room then, her eyes narrowing toward Melanie as though she were physically inspecting the officer's words.

'Do you think that matters?' the bereaved mother whispered. 'Do you think it matters to us the tiniest jot whether you reek bloody vengeance on the animal that did this?' She became increasingly louder with each word. 'Someone has snatched our daughter away, Detective. Frankly, I couldn't care less if the world stopped spinning entirely, never mind if you catch the monster behind this bloody madness. She's our daughter.' Evie's breath staggered, and she leaned heavily into her husband, as though another wave of grief had descended on her. 'She was our daughter, Rob,' she spoke into her husband's chest before giving way to another round of tears, these more ferocious than the last.

Dixon appeared in the doorway of the room. He smiled a hello to Melanie and stepped toward the couple seated in the right-hand side of the living space. Crouching down in front of them both, he introduced himself and his purpose.

'I'm going to be here, round the clock if you'd like me to be, and you can think of me as your direct line to everything that's happening in the investigation.' Evie Grantham held eye contact with the officer as he spoke; it was the most engaged the mother had looked in some minutes. 'If you have questions, concerns, if you remember something that might be important, if you need milk or butter, I'm here.'

Melanie stood to greet Carter in the doorway.

'I'm so sorry for your loss,' the DS directed his sympathies to Robert, given that Evie was absorbed in a quiet conversation with the crouching Dixon.

'Thank you, officers.'

'I'm sorry to ask, Mr Grantham, but might we have a look around Jenni's room while we're here? There are certain things that might be

C.S. BARNES

useful, and it's best that we find them sooner...' Watton trailed off as Robert again held up a hand to pause her.

'Do what you need to do, Detective, you'll have no arguments from us.'

Seconds later, trailing his boss up the stairs to Jenni's room, Carter whispered, 'That's the hard part over at least.'

'Don't be a rookie, Edd,' Melanie snapped. 'The hard part hasn't even started.'

6

DS Edd Carter rubbed hard at his eyes, straightened his tie, and practiced a smile before launching himself out of his car and up the driveway of his family home. As he reached for the doorbell, the front door opened to reveal a near-silhouette of his mother, backlit by the warmth of the hallway. She smiled and stepped aside for him to come in, and he stopped to plant a kiss on her cheek as he entered. The two made their way quietly into the kitchen and Carter's mother clicked the door closed before speaking.

'Long day again, love?' She crossed the room to the kettle. Edd's father was sitting at the small table in the centre of the space, so engrossed in his paper that he hadn't yet looked up to acknowledge his son.

'It has been, yeah.' Edd pulled out a chair and dropped himself down opposite his dad. 'You alright behind there, old man?' His father nodded without making eye contact and from behind him Edd saw his mother shake her head lightly while making the tea.

It wasn't until she'd finished the task and set three cups on the table that Edd's father rested his paper to one side, let out a sharp cough, and said, 'What's going on, lad?'

Edd looked to his mother for clarification, but she seemed as ready for an answer as his father was.

'I don't know what you mean.'

'Love.' His mother's tone was softer than the old man's at least. 'We've had Emily nearly every night this last week, and we don't mind.' She squeezed her husband's hand deliberately, strengthening his silence, Edd guessed. 'We don't mind at all because she's a little star, she really is. But she's said some things while she's been here that's got us–'

'Has Trish left?' Edd's father snapped, and his wife shot him a look that could floor a man. He merely shrugged. 'You'll be dancing round the houses, and I've got a paper to finish,' he said pointedly to his wife before turning to his son again. 'The lass hasn't seen or heard from her mother, and there's no one there to collect her from school, so something's occurring that you're not telling us about.'

Edd sighed. Just like that, he was thirteen again. He'd been caught bunking off school and his mother was gently encouraging him to admit to the crime. Meanwhile his dad blurted out what the crime was and how Edd would be punished for it. It had always been their way; the ballerina and the steamroller, Edd thought, not that he'd ever really minded. It had often been quite a comfort being able to predict his parents' behaviours so well; although the general state of his home life meant that he'd been blindsided by this confrontation in a way that he hadn't been before. He took a large gulp of hot tea, set the cup down and said, 'Trish left about a week ago, yeah.' His mother's hand flew to her mouth as a shocked gasp slipped out, while his father simply nodded for his son to continue. 'She said she needed some time away and when I asked how long, she said she'd have to let me know, and I haven't heard from her since. I've tried to talk to her, sent a few texts, called once or twice, but nothing.'

His mother stood. 'You're a police officer, for God's sake. Aren't you concerned?'

'That something has happened to her?'

'Yes, Edward, that something has happened to her.' His mother's tone cut through him.

'She's fine, Mum. She's using social media; I know where she is,' Edd offered by way of reassurance but his mother merely shook her head, narrowed her eyes, and carried her tea back to the kitchen counter. Facing away from both men, she threw the hot contents of the mug into the sink and slammed down the cup on the sideboard before turning back to them.

'And what about her daughter?' she demanded. 'Where does she fit in?'

'I'm looking after Emily for the foreseeable,' Edd replied.

'Except you aren't; we are!'

His mother burst out of the room in a fashion that Edd thought was a touch dramatic, and his father's eye roll suggested he felt the same. The two men sat in silence for an uncomfortable amount of time. Edd's father sipped at his tea and stared down one corner of the table, as though deep in thought. Given his mother's reaction to the news, he was braced for a reprimand of some kind from his father too.

'Did anything happen?' his dad finally asked.

Edd shrugged. 'From my end, we're the same as we've always been. I'm working a bit more, since the promotion, but we both knew that would happen, and it's not like we're not being compensated for it; there's more money coming in, we're more comfortable.' He paused to consider this. 'I thought we were more comfortable. Trish obviously has other ideas on the matter.' He stared into his tea, as though he might find an answer to the messy situation somewhere at the bottom of his mug.

'Women, they're tricky,' his father said. 'Do you think there's someone else?'

It was a thought Edd had entertained every hour on the hour since his wife had left. He knew roughly where she was staying, but not who with, nor how she was affording it, given that their joint account hadn't suffered much of a dent. But he had no evidence for there being another person involved, no. He shook his head but held his glare on the cooling drink in front of him; this confrontation was hard enough without having to look his father in the eye too. Without another word, his father stood up from his seat and closed the distance between them; standing just behind Edd, the older man set a firm hand on his son's shoulder and gave a reassuring squeeze.

'This isn't on you, lad. Your mother, she's tricky and all, but she'll see this isn't on you.' His in- and exhale that followed sounded shaky, and Edd thought that if he turned he might catch his father on the cusp of tears. For this reason, he stayed facing straight ahead. His dad gave another squeeze of his shoulder before he stepped away and moved towards the door, visible in Edd's peripherals. 'We'll tend to Emily for a night or two, and I'll check on your mother. You stay here for as long as you like, alright?' He didn't wait for an answer, just shut the door gently behind him, leaving Edd alone with his cold tea and those on-the-hour thoughts.

DI Melanie Watton kicked the front door closed behind her. She thumbed through the collection of bills that had been waiting for her in her letterbox and continued on her way to the kitchen. There was a casserole dish of cold pasta on the middle shelf of her too-big-for-one-person fridge that she retrieved, and with a fork and no bowl, she ate directly from the large container while ripping through her post.

After four large mouthfuls of food, she replaced the pasta with a bottle of alcohol-free beer. She took two large gulps of the stuff and winced as it went down; not drinking on work nights was a house rule. The officer padded back to the hallway to collect her work bag and heaved it onto the dining room table. She pulled out the same brown folder that she'd taken with her to the Grantham house earlier in the day.

Robert Grantham had been quick to collect together additional photographs of his daughter – 'For news reports, maybe, or appeals, or whatever it is,' he'd explained, and Melanie had nodded, accepted the photographs, and stashed them away for safekeeping. They lay scattered across Melanie's wooden table top; a timeline of the girl from what Melanie guessed was around fourteen, judging from the school uniform, all the way through to college – a recent photograph taken from a drama production – and, eventually, to death. The image of Jenni's pale face against the steel of the examination table lay at the far end of the timeline. Melanie pulled it closer towards her, took another swig of fake-beer, and balanced the image upright against the centrepiece of the table.

The minutes slipped by as Melanie stared at each image in turn, but the timeline soon overwhelmed her. There was a newsagents ten minutes away that would be open, she thought, and they would surely be selling beer. Melanie locked her front door behind her but left the lights on, and the splay of images across her dining room table, ready for her return.

DC Chris Burton had been sitting in her car outside her own house for close on twenty minutes when her mobile rang. Joe's number displayed across the screen.

He spoke as soon as she answered. 'Are you going to stay out there all night?'

Chris let out a long exhale. 'It was a kid, Joe. She was just a kid.'

Joe didn't respond but held a comforting silence as Chris watched him cross from the living room window to the front door. The door opened, letting out the welcoming light of their hallway.

'You can come in and talk about it, or not talk about it at all,' Joe said, leaning against the doorframe.

Chris loved her job, she always had done, but there were some days when everything was just too much. Seeing a young girl's life extinguished decades too soon was a lot for anyone to bear and while Chris had handled it fine on the surface – she knew better than to let appearances slip at work – now she was home she knew that her feelings were in danger of spilling out.

'I don't think I want to talk,' she eventually replied, letting her head drop against the seat behind her. 'Is that okay?'

'Of course it is. Dinner's nearly ready, so I'll go and dish up, but I won't say a word,' Joe said before ending their call. He disappeared from the doorway, leaving the door open enough for a small crack of light to fall through.

Chris stayed in the car for a minute or two longer.

7

DC Chris Burton entered the incident room with a nervous stomach the following morning. She walked past her back-row colleagues and positioned herself on a seat at the front of the room. The DI had sent round an early message asking people to attend a team meeting, and Chris was grateful that she'd managed to get to the office on time – earlier than others, by the looks of things too.

As the latecomers filtered in, accompanied by one or two uniformed officers, Chris took a look around the room for DS Edd Carter. He wasn't at his desk or loitering by the coffee machine, and after checking these places, Chris found herself hard pushed for somewhere else to look.

Behind Chris, DI Melanie Watton's door swung open with a force and out came the DI herself, closely followed by Carter who gave Chris a quick smile before taking a seat next to her.

'Did I miss something?' she whispered.

'Not here,' he replied.

Melanie called attention to the room of bodies before her. 'Eyes front, folks. We've got some news.'

'Good news?' DC David Read leapt on Melanie's opening remark and she answered him with a stern expression. Read held both hands flat and facing forward in a pose of surrender until his superior had swung round to face the whiteboard behind her.

In large letters above the victim shot, Melanie wrote: JENNI GRANTHAM. Beneath this she wrote the victim's age, her parents' names, the name of her college, and the two friends that were known associates of hers. Capping the pen, Melanie turned to face her team.

'This is what we know.' She allowed a second for her colleagues to process the information. 'Where we go next is the big question. A retrieval crew will be going to the Grantham home at some point today to collect together various items belonging to the victim: laptop, tablet, her mobile phone if anyone can find the thing, although to date it seems that's a washout.'

'Might the killer have it?' Read interrupted. 'A kind of souvenir?'

'It's a thought,' Melanie agreed. 'But until we know more about the case, we can't make that kind of assumption, so keep your eyes out where you can; it may still be in the public sphere somewhere, it's just a case of finding it. Alongside the retrieval team, DC Morris...' Melanie raised her voice to pull in the young officer's attention. 'I want you to chase up CCTV. There aren't loads of cameras around the playing fields area, but she got there from one route or another and I want a better idea of which route she was taking and who she was taking it with, assuming the field is our murder scene. Failing that, look out for footage of anyone acting suspicious, carrying anything suspicious.'

Morris looked up from her notebook. 'Suspicious?'

'You know, like someone carrying a body for instance,' DC Brian Fairer bit back, to the amusement of several of his teammates, and the young woman dropped her head toward her notebook. Melanie hoped she wasn't writing down what Fairer had just said.

'Another area that we need covered is the college itself,' Melanie picked up. 'DS Carter, I want you and DC Burton to head over there and make the principal aware of the situation. Rumours are already flying and we're just about managing to keep Jenni's name from the press, so we need to get information out there officially before we lose control over it. My advice would be to pin him down on some interviews, starting with the kids that Evie Grantham told us about. If there's a problem, have their parents called in.' Carter and Burton nodded in unison, and Melanie switched her attention to the back of the room.

'I believe we have two visitors to address the room now?' The DI spoke to the uniformed officers at the back of the crowd. One of them looked delighted to have been called upon by a superior officer, while the other looked as though he might vomit over the evidence box that occupied his lap. 'You're welcome to come up to the front to address the team,' Melanie invited, and the more enthusiastic of the two bounded through the room and stood proudly in front of the whiteboard. He was already addressing the team as a whole when his less-confident colleague joined him, evidence box in tow.

'We were part of the team left to search the fields after the... after Jenni's body.' He paused here and looked to Melanie for approval before starting again. 'It was a bit out of the way, but we spotted something that caught our eye.' Giving the nod to his nervous associate, the other uniformed officer pulled evidence bags out of the box and spread them across the table in front of the whiteboard. 'It's a set of clothes, some of which shows the logo of Jenni's college. But it doesn't have a name or anything in it.' He paused, as though this were his big punchline, but laughed lightly as he realised something. 'Sorry, it did have a name in it, that's the point. There are signs of a clothing tag that have been snipped out, but someone left behind the ends that were sewn in.' The young officer shrugged lightly and held out his hands in a there-you-have-it gesture and Melanie thanked them for their contribution to the case; although she wasn't quite sure how they'd spotted the missing name tag on their brief look over the items. Either way, it was good information to have – as long as it hadn't led to any contaminated evidence along the way.

Melanie waited until the two junior officers had exited the room before she continued her address of the team. 'While we still can't jump to conclusions, this might be the beginning of an answer for why Jenni was dressed to look much older than she was. Either she dressed like this voluntarily for some reason; Evie Grantham did say that Jenni and her friends were having a Halloween run-through, which begs the question of what her costume was. However, there is the other option which is that our killer changed her into these clothes, either before or after the murder, presumably to make her look older, or even to make her look like someone else.' Melanie rubbed hard at her temples; she was beginning to drown in her own variables and, for a case that was still in its infancy, she felt frustrated by how little they had to go on in order to get this investigation off the ground.

'What chance do we stand of working out which of those options is right, boss?' Carter intervened, sounding much more sceptical than he'd intended.

Melanie shrugged. 'George might be able to tell if there's been heavy manipulation of the body post-mortem; if she was dead when the killer dressed her, it won't have been an easy feat. But asking around at the college is another good place to start with this too; if they were doing a Halloween test-run, start by asking Jenni's friends what she was planning to dress up as. Until then, does everyone know what they're doing for the day ahead?'

A chorus of non-committed grunts arose from her tired audience, and Melanie dismissed them shortly after. She was heading back towards her own office when she crossed paths with Burton.

'Got a second?' the DI asked her junior and Chris nodded, following her boss into the private office space. 'Shut the door, would you?' Melanie asked. While Chris tended to this, Melanie walked to one of several filing cabinets that stood tall at the back of the room, taking over much of the wall. She retrieved a dark green shirt, creased but fresh smelling, and laid it out on her desk. The gesture was met with a frown from Chris so Melanie leaned forward with an outstretched index finger, pointing to a thumbprint of grease on her colleague's shirt.

Chris smiled. 'Joe insisted on breakfast. Crumpets.'

'You've got a good one there,' Melanie said. 'I'm just going to turn around while you put the shirt on, and then you can head out.' She smiled and faced away from her junior, allowing her some privacy.

Within a minute or two, the office door creaked open again and Chris stepped outside, but she leaned back into the room and added, 'Thanks, boss.'

'Any time,' Melanie replied, but Chris had already gone.

8

The building looked like a lovechild between a school and a prison; despite the *Welcome* sign that sat outside the gates, there was something unfriendly about the college's exterior. DS Edd Carter shuddered at the sight of the place and DC Chris Burton nodded in silent agreement.

Unable to drive straight into the grounds, they had parked their unmarked vehicle down the street and walked the rest of the way. They found that the entrance gates, including the walkway entrance, were locked, and the only way to gain access was to buzz through the intercom fixed to a squat pillar alongside the steel railings. These seemed like desperate measures for a well-to-do college to take, Chris thought, but she kept quiet while her partner held his thumb down on the intercom button and waited for it to connect.

'What do you think of the place?' Carter asked, nodding to the building. 'It doesn't look too bright and cheery, does it.'

'Does school ever?' Burton replied.

'Fair point.' Edd buzzed again. 'Aren't there supposed to be people–?'

'Hello!' The sound startled both officers and, for the first time that day, they managed to crack a slight smile. 'Hello, sorry for the wait, how may I help you?'

'We're DS Carter and DC Burton; we called ahead to speak to Mr...' Carter hesitated.

'Gibbons,' Chris filled the blank.

The intercom clicked and the gates behind the officers slowly opened, as though laden with hesitation at letting them inside. Burton tried not to be offended by the curt dismissal of the intercom's operative, but as first impressions went, the college wasn't doing much for her so far. She treaded up the drive toward the front entrance, walking level with Carter.

When they reached the door, it opened before either had the chance to reach for the handle, and they were greeted by the sight of a tall older gentleman, respectable looking, and obviously expecting them. Without a word, he stepped aside for the two officers to join him inside the building, and only when the door was shut did he extend a hand and an introduction.

'Mr Gibbons, pleased to meet you both.' He shook Carter's hand firmly, assertively, and gave a curt nod to Burton, which she matched; she couldn't help but be put out by not getting her own handshake, although it was something she should have gotten used to. 'Terrible circumstances, of course, but nevertheless. The students are aware that you're here, but might we step inside my office first, before we bring them into the discussion?' The officers agreed but Burton didn't go easily; there was something unsettling about the man, and it wasn't just his misplaced old-boy façade that was throwing her. As the college principal stepped ahead of them to guide them to the correct room, Carter and Burton shot each other a look that confirmed they were on the same page in their thinking.

'Is this a private college, Mr Gibbons?' Burton asked as the office door closed behind her. She took a seat next to her partner, opposite the principal with the healthy span of an oversized desk between them.

Gibbons considered the question. 'No, I wouldn't say so. We're government funded, but we have a reputation for turning out good apples from bad seeds.' He followed this with a picture-perfect smile that left Burton wondering whether he'd ripped this line straight from one of the college's brochures.

'You have some troublesome students?' she pushed.

'Not for long,' Gibbons replied, with a hint of that same too-wide smile.

'And you mentioned that you had students ready for us,' Carter picked up.

'Yes, after your superior, DI Watton, was it?' Gibbons clarified. The DI had called ahead to discuss arrangements for speaking to the students before sending her best DS and DC over for this chat. There were rumours in the local newspapers already and, with a missing college girl and a newly discovered body both occupying front pages, it didn't take long for the two stories to become inter-twined. 'She explained that you're investigating the death of one of our students.'

The DI hadn't had the time to tell her colleagues how much Gibbons knew, but Burton was grateful they didn't have to break the news of Jenni Grantham's passing.

Gibbons continued. 'Naturally, I've made the students in her year aware of the situation and they're all deeply saddened, but also very eager to help.'

Chris made a note of something and nodded for Edd to continue.

'Might we ask you one or two questions about Jenni first?'

'Please do.'

'What sort of student was she? Attentive, reliable?' Edd fired the question and Chris remained poised to capture any answers they were given. Jenni's parents had said nothing but good things about their daughter, naturally, and while the team understood that, it didn't exactly help them to build their case. 'Was she a troublemaker?' Edd added, noting Gibbons' hesitation.

'No,' the man admitted slowly. 'But she certainly didn't mind spending her time with troublemakers, particularly in the last two or three weeks, I'd say.'

'Any names jump out at you that might be worth us talking to?' Edd pushed again.

Gibbons considered for a moment. 'Eleanor Gregory is a name to listen out for, I'd say. Where you find her, you'll usually find quite a gaggle, including some of our male students too.' He paused and held the silence until Chris stopped writing. 'You'll have the chance to meet these students for yourselves, of course, but Caroline Smith is another name to write down, as is Patrick Nelson. While you're at it, listen out for Alistair House.'

'Are these all associates of Jenni Grantham's?' Carter asked.

'Largely. Alistair is a bit of an outcast in the class, but it had come to my attention recently that he had something of a thing for the Grantham girl.'

'What makes you say that?' Chris asked, pausing her writing to pick at this new thread.

'Generally speaking, our students pick their subjects and they stick to them. Jenni was having a hard time working out university choices though, which meant that she was sampling a number of classes. It could well be a coincidence,' he said, using a tone that suggested it was no coincidence at all. 'But Alistair has logged and retracted three course change forms in the last five weeks, and they coincide with when Jenni would have been trying different classes.' Gibbons rubbed at his temples and gave a short, sharp laugh. 'He was following her around the college in many ways, or trying to at least.'

'Did Jenni speak with you directly about this, or any other members of staff?' Chris asked, still making notes from Gibbons' most recent admission.

'Not me, no, and not to any other teachers that I'm aware of.'

'No official reports were made then?' Edd tried to clarify but Gibbons broke through the question with another curt laugh.

'Detectives, good grief. I'm sure there's nothing to be concerned about, it just seemed like something you should know. Boys will be boys after all, won't they.'

Edd and Chris exchanged a look; yes, boys will be boys, and that's precisely what both detectives were concerned about.

9

The desk was a mess of faded photographs, printed transcripts and handwritten notes; accompanied by the documents that had somehow made it onto the digital system midway through the Michael Richards case, which were lined up in open tabs on DI Melanie Watton's aging desktop monitor. She had been reading for nearly two hours and she was yet to find something that could explain the arrival of a copycat killer. The murders had all been heavily reported and Richards had made the most of this catapult into fame, offering various newspapers a number of exclusives long after he was sentenced to life in prison. But what had happened *now* to trigger this new killer?

Melanie pulled up a fresh search window and typed in Richards' full name. As she'd suspected, the local newspapers had been quiet, especially around the news of Richards' death. But the national newspapers were a different story. There was an influx of headlines centred around the killer's recent demise, with some even going as far to state that he deserved what had happened to him. "What goes around..." seemed to be the gist of many articles and, while Melanie might agree off the record, she shook her head in disapproval at the sight of so many bloodthirsty civilians. Curiosity alone pulled her into the online comments attached to the articles, and here public opinion only worsened.

Thestateofthings:
I'd have done the same myself given half the chance

Murdermostfoul:
Who can blame them i'd murder someone for killing my sister

Britainbornanbread:
Thank fuck I'm not wasting my taxes keepin him any longer

The comments went on and on until Melanie couldn't stand to look at them any longer. She back-clicked to the search engine's home-page and tried to clear her mind of the online vitriol. It made no sense, seeing so much unashamed hate towards a man that someone was imitating. Unless the new killer wasn't imitating Richards at all. The frustration of these new ideas built and built until Melanie dropped her fist against the desk with a mighty thump. She needed George Waller's findings from the post-mortem of the victim, but she knew from experience that calling George before he was good and ready to talk would only delay matters further in the long run.

Perfectly timed, her mobile phone vibrated across the desk causing a burst of noise inside her small office. Melanie snatched at the handset without even checking the caller's ID.

'Watton.'

'Boss, it's me,' DS Carter started, and Melanie couldn't help but sigh into the speaker. 'We're at the college still but we wanted to run something by you.' Melanie grabbed a pen and a fresh sheet of paper, prepared for whatever was coming. 'There's a kid here who's been taking a keen interest in Jenni, by all accounts. Alistair House, his name is. He's only Jenni's age–'

'Too young to be in the big boy system but there might be something kicking around,' Melanie said, finishing her colleague's theory. 'I'll get the team onto it, see if they can find any family connections or anything similar that might lead somewhere. Thanks, Edd.'

'No problem. We're going in to talk to Jenni's year group. We'll let you know when we're heading back.'

The pair extinguished their phone call without the formality of a goodbye, and Melanie begrudgingly pulled herself back to the open case files in front of her. She chose Victim Number One, Zoe Ingram, from the pile and looked over the folder's contents. The killing was unmotivated; there was never any proven link between Zoe and the man who murdered her, nor could Richards provide the police with one, despite repeated questioning on the matter. All his victims were selected at random, he maintained, but there was nothing too random about the beauty and youth that he targeted. Melanie picked over the collection of photographs from Zoe's file; noting how the first four showed her alive, happy, surrounded by friends in some and family in others. The last picture showed her face, close-up, with that same steel examination table visible in the background.

The accompanying case files for victims two to five were much the same, with the addition of Richards' handwritten notes that became increasingly antagonistic as the killings continued. In the final folder that she opened, she found typed transcripts of conversations between Richards and a number of different detectives from the case. They were as unpleasant a read as the case files to date had been, showing a cocksure Richards who was clearly hell-bent on winding up the detectives who were interrogating him. A few pages along, Melanie was pulled into one of the final transcribed conversations where Richards explained – or, tried to explain – his reasoning for committing the five murders.

Richards: Everyone knows who I am now, don't they?

DI Ewen: And that's why you did, is it, so everyone would know your name?

Richards: You're saying it like it's stupid, but it's worked, hasn't it? That's why I had to hand myself in too. Frankly, you lot were taking a bit too long to get around to finding me. Even though I made it easy for you. (laughter) Hey ho, we're all here now.

DI Ewen: You understand that you've killed people, Mr Richards, you've ruined lives of young women who didn't deserve it.

Richards: Oh, c'mon. They weren't so innocent. They wouldn't have been out on the playing fields at all hours with a boy like me if they had been. They took their chances just like everyone does –

There was a hard tap of knuckles against Melanie's office door, and she'd never been more grateful for an interruption. She closed the transcript and shouted her permission through to whoever was outside. The door inched open and DC Lucy Morris hovered nervously on the threshold to the office. The DI gestured her in with one hand while reshuffling the documents with the other. When Melanie looked up, Lucy was still a metre away from the desk edge, what she obviously considered to be a safe distance from her superior officer.

'Let's have it,' Melanie snapped.

'The tech team has had a chance to look through Jenni Grantham's computer.' Melanie's impatience gave way to optimism at the mere thought of a break in the case; the young DC had her full attention. 'Her web browsing history, it's mostly random searches and social media websites, nothing too remarkable yet,' Lucy continued, reading from the sheet in front of her. 'But there were a handful of searches that grabbed some attention; she's been looking into Michael Richards, particularly in the two weeks before her murder.' She paused here and passed the piece of paper over to her superior who snatched it from her with the excitement of a hungry child. Melanie inspected the sheet. 'They've noted down the specific search terms for us there.'

Melanie scanned the list: Michael Richards murders, Michael Richards picture, Michael Richards victims, Michael Richards victim clothing...

'Shit,' Melanie muttered as she reached the bottom of the list. 'Is there anything else on there that we should know about?' She looked to her colleague as she spoke.

Lucy nodded. 'They're arranging for copies of her most recent conversations through her social media channels and through her emails, so we'll have those to go through before the day is out. They've said they'll flag anything else of interest as it comes up, so there might be one or two surprises still to come.'

'If this is anything to go by.' Melanie gestured to the sheet in front of her. 'Are you okay to take point on this?' Lucy flashed a quick smile in confirmation, showing what Melanie thought must be pride. 'You know what you're looking for; if anything does come through, anything at all, flag it and raise it with me.' Melanie dismissed the young officer with a thank you and a thin smile, and Lucy gratefully retreated, closing the door behind her. 'Jenni, Jenni, Jenni,' Melanie said, scanning the search terms a second time. 'What on earth were you getting yourself into?'

10

DS Edd Carter stepped into the room ahead of his colleague, so he was the first out of the two of them to be greeted by the intimidating sight of thirty-seven pairs of eyes staring at him in unison. Edd was visibly unnerved, but when DC Chris Burton straightened up alongside him, she showed no such concern with the gang of students. Seconds later, Mr Gibbons followed and positioned himself behind the desk at the head of the room, in front of what looked to be an interactive whiteboard. When Chris turned again to eye the principal, she came face to face with an enhanced image of their victim. Jenni Grantham's face occupied much of the board space behind Chris and Edd, and it was a startling sight to behold. She nudged Edd to pull his attention to the same image, but he was fixed on the students, a hare in headlights.

Gibbons cleared his throat. 'You're all aware of the tragedy that has taken place in our local community, and I know this is a difficult time for many of you.' Edd and Chris took this opportunity to scan around the room, watching for tearful reactions, hoping – sick as it sounded – for some early signs of guilt. 'The police are doing everything that they can to decipher what happened to Jenni, but your help in the matter will go a long way.'

Despite Chris not having taken to Gibbons during their earlier conversation, she couldn't deny that he clearly had a good hold over his students. Every one of them was held in the principal's address and the room remained pin-drop quiet while he continued. 'I know not everyone knew Jenni, and not everyone will have spent that much time with her; you're a large group and all that. But if you know of anything that could be useful, now is the time to speak out.' Gibbons eyed the student body, as though waiting for a hand to shoot in the air and offer the right answer; *I know, I know, I know who killed her...* Chris only wished it could be that easy.

When an uncomfortable minute had rolled by, the DS decided to intervene. 'I know this is a horrible time for a lot of people here, and we're interested in making this as swift as possible because we appreciate that this is very difficult.' He turned then to address the principal directly. 'I assume there are some people here who didn't know Jenni especially well, is that right?'

'Of course, they're a large class,' Gibbons replied.

'Perhaps it might be worth narrowing down the numbers?' Burton added, finishing her partner's line of thought. She turned to address the group herself. 'If you knew Jenni, or you spent time with her during the weeks before her death, could you please remain seated. If you didn't, you're welcome to leave.' The numbers dwindled significantly, and Carter appeared to immediately relax at the decrease. When a small queue of teenagers was left to trail out of the door, a curt shout emerged from the back of the room.

'House, where do you think you're going?'

Chris and Edd shot a synchronised stare at the open doorway to find a young man about to cross the threshold. When Chris looked back to find the source of the noise, she spotted a young woman, out of her seat and staring with some accusation at the startled boy who she'd beckoned.

'You were round her like a sniffer dog so sit down,' the same young woman said before taking her own seat. With some evident despondency, the young man slouched back to his table without making eye contact with anyone along the way.

Gibbons had requested to be present during the police discussion with the pupils – which seemed only fair, given that he had helped them to side-step calling each set of parents for permission. So, students seated and ready, Carter closed the door before rejoining his partner at the head of the class.

Burton started the discussion. 'Who in this room was with Jenni on the night she was killed?'

One hand raised in an instant; a second, more hesitant, hand followed this.

'Ellie,' the confident student – the one who had called House out on his sudden exit, Chris saw – introduced herself without being prompted. 'This is Patrick,' she said, gesturing to the less confident student sitting next to her. 'We were with her the evening it happened.' She spoke with such confidence that Chris found herself jarred by the teenager's composure. Meanwhile, the young man to Ellie's left showed no such control.

'Eleanor Gregory and Patrick Nelson?' Edd chimed in, reading from the list Gibbons had provided for them already.

Ellie smiled. 'You've heard of us.'

Edd went to speak but Chris set a hand on his arm to halt him. 'What were you two doing on the night of Jenni's...' She hesitated over the phrasing. 'On the night of the incident? Were the three of you up to something in particular?'

'We were practising Halloween costumes,' Ellie replied, still with that same confidence.

'A trial run?' Chris asked.

'Exactly.'

'What were you dressing up as?' Chris smiled to soften the question.

'I was Freddy,' Ellie said, matching Chris's smile.

The DC felt like the entire conversation was out of place, as was the young woman's willingness to take part in it. Chris looked around to catch Edd's eye and, from his frowned expression, she thought he was thinking much the same as she was.

'And your friend, Patrick, who were you?' Chris aimed the question directly at the young man, fixing him with a stare, but still it was Ellie who replied.

'He was Jason.' She seemed pleased by their plan, as though she were the first person to think of this costume pairing. 'You know, Freddy versus Jason,' she pushed, apparently displeased with the neutral reaction that Chris had given her.

'And who was Jenni?'

As though flicking a switch, Chris watched the confidence drain out of the young woman in front of her. Ellie looked as though she were physically deflating as she sank further into her seat and, for the first time since their conversation had started, she dropped her eye contact with the questioning officer. The young woman flashed a glance at Patrick, who was slumped in a similar position next to her; the two shared something, but Chris couldn't decipher what. Were they a couple? Or were they accomplices?

Before she had the time to interrogate the thought properly, Patrick finally made eye contact with her and said, 'A victim.' His voice cracked mid-way through his speech, so he said it again, as though wanting to be sure. 'For Halloween, Jenni was dressing up as someone's victim.'

11

Robert Grantham pulled the phone line from the connection port in the wall and checked that his wife's mobile, and his own, were switched off. DI Watton had assured him that the police would deliver any news in person, rather than over the phone, and so the bereaved father thought it was time to shut himself off from the world – and the news-hungry journalists who occupied it. DC Ian Dixon had been a godsend in the days since Jenni's death, but there was only so much he could do about the harassing phone calls and the unsolicited offers of help from people who knew nothing about the case – who knew nothing about Jenni.

'Why do they keep calling?' Robert had asked Dixon one evening, when his wife had long dropped off into a drug-induced sleep, and the two men were left alone with a pot of tea and the remains of another casserole, delivered by a neighbour earlier in the day.

Dixon shrugged. 'It's a horrible world, Robert, and I'm afraid some people are just too eager to capitalise on that.'

Robert had managed to go another hour or two after that, but he soon found himself desperate to shut off means of communications entirely.

. . .

'What if someone wants us?' Evie asked when she came downstairs in the morning to find their three house phones disconnected and piled together on the dining room table.

'Who in the world could want us, Evie? The only person who did has gone.'

'That's not true, Rob, it just isn't. What if...' She trailed off, unable to finish her own sentence, and while her husband in part wanted to shout at her, he instead moved across the dining room and encased her in a warm hug. Evie's shoulders sagged, and Robert soon felt the wetness of tears pressing through the front of his shirt; he matched them with a handful of his own stray tears, landing on his wife's bowed head. These moments – these shared moments of outpouring – felt to Robert like the only things holding them together, although he hadn't said such concerns to his wife, or even Dixon.

The shriek of the doorbell rang through the house, cutting short the couple's contact. Evie pulled away, a confused expression on her face, meanwhile her husband showed contempt, even a flicker of anger. He pushed past Evie and padded out into the hallway, to find Dixon poised to open the front door already.

'If that's a journalist, you tell them where to go,' Robert instructed and Dixon nodded his understanding, although he was unlikely to follow the guidance to the letter.

The young officer indicated for Robert to go back inside before he turned to open the door himself. But there was no one waiting. The journalists who had been spending their days outside of the Granthams' house hadn't even arrived yet. From this angle, the street looked normal and deserted of human presence. The only giveaway that anyone had been to the house at all was the large box that sat on the doorstep, taped together in an obviously clumsy fashion – either by someone inexperienced or someone who was rushing. In block capitals someone had written *FAO Granthams* across the top of the container.

Dixon remained inside the house but crouched down in the open doorway. He pulled his phone from his back pocket and hit the speed dial for DI Watton's work phone number. She answered after two rings, as though she had been waiting for the call.

'Dixon?'

'I'm sorry to call you so early, Ma'am. There's a package at the Granthams' house. Marked for their attention but it was hand delivered, and whoever dropped it off had ducked out before I got to the front door.'

Melanie expelled a shaky sigh. 'Christ. Okay, I'll call it in. Don't touch a thing, Dixon, and don't let the Granthams either.'

Melanie disconnected the phone call and, still pulling on her work attire, dialled out to the other team leaders...

12

DS Edd Carter stood at the front of the incident room with his team – Melanie's team, that is – staring back at him. His boss had called just thirty minutes earlier to tell him she was on her way to the Grantham residence to help with investigations into a package that had been left on their doorstep.

'What kind of package?' Edd asked.

Melanie sighed. 'That's the question, isn't it.'

The DI had asked him to take the lead on the meeting for the morning, to fill the team in on his and Chris's discoveries at the school, and to see where other people were in their own investigations. But before he could do any of that, he had to get the team to take him seriously with a custard stain smudged down the front of his shirt.

'What even is it?' DC David Read shouted from the back.

'It's a sign that I've got kids, now can we?' Edd batted back, and the back row sniggered like self-important school children. 'I'm happy you're in a top mood this morning but if you could channel some of that energy into finding out who murdered Jenni Grantham, you'd be doing the rest of us a solid favour.' Edd spoke pointedly at

Read, whose laughter quickly died out on hearing his superior's tone.

Read didn't offer an apology but sank an inch or two lower in his seat, and he wore a similar sad face to the one Emily tried out when she knew that she was in trouble. But if it didn't work when Carter's own daughter did it, Read stood no chance. 'Okay, updates,' the DS started again. 'DC Morris?'

The officer stood up to address the group. 'I've been working with the tech team to sift through Jenni's recent Internet searches. From what we've seen so far, it looks as though she was taking an interest in the Michael Richards case.'

'What kind of an interest?' DC Fairer asked before Edd could.

'She did a lot of searches on the victims, actually.' Morris shuffled through papers as she spoke. 'She seems to have been looking for pictures of the victims, their clothing when they were attacked, things like that.' She looked back to her DS. 'No surprises, but it turns out she was quite an active Internet user, so even though we've searched through a fair amount of data, there's still a fair bit to go. These victim searches are the most significant things we've found so far, but we haven't started on her emails yet...' The DC trailed off, throwing a nervous look in Edd's direction before sitting back down. For as long as she had worked with the team, Morris had come across as jumpy, edgy, and Edd had never been able to work out why. He shook away these recurring thoughts though; now wasn't the time to overanalyse his team mates.

'Okay, good work,' Edd said, trying to mimic the soft support that Melanie would have offered. 'Funnily enough, Burton and I found our own victim connection at Jenni's college yesterday. Chris?' He invited her to present their findings.

Chris moved to the front of the room and grabbed a board marker on her way. On the white surface behind her, she wrote: *Gibbons, Eleanor Gregory, Patrick Nelson,* and *Alistair House.* She circled Gibbons' name. 'College principal, stuck up, thinks his students are little shits but also believes he can change them. We had a good chat with Mr Gibbons ahead of talking to the students themselves and he introduced us to the name Alistair House.' She paused to circle this name. 'It looks as though he had a major thing for our victim, he was class swapping to try to spend some more time with her, that sort of thing. But the most interesting piece of information yesterday came from these two.'

She paused again and sketched a messy line linking Eleanor and Patrick together on the board. 'These were, as far as we know, the last two people to see Jenni alive. They were at Eleanor's house doing a dress rehearsal for Halloween. When we asked for details of their costumes, Ellie told us that her and Patrick were pairing up as Freddy and Jason from the horror films, meanwhile Jenni...' Chris crossed to the other side of the board where Jenni's pictures were pinned. Chris underlined the victim's name. 'Jenni's Halloween costume was a victim.'

A murmur of something – confusion? – travelled around the team, resulting in a final outburst from Read. 'A victim? A victim of what?'

Newspaper clippings spilled from the box like lifeless confetti. The package had been inspected by the station's resident explosives expert and opened carefully by forensics. DI Melanie Watton was sifting through, her gloved hands wading through one news article at a time, many of which dated back years to the original Michael Richards' killings. There were newspaper profiles of the victims, ranging from the early reveal of their identities to later anniversaries of their deaths, and there were several interviews with Richards himself that had been dissected into smaller snippets, so Watton found them one paragraph at a time as she continued her search.

The papers were spread across the Granthams' dining room table, meanwhile the couple were being detained in their living room, with DC Dixon offering them lukewarm explanations for what was happening one room over. Melanie didn't envy him the job.

'Zach?' the DI said quietly, pulling back the attention of the forensics officer who had been dispatched to help her. They'd worked together before – closely enough to be on a first name basis – and she was grateful to have someone she could trust handling such delicate evidence. The man – gloved, aproned, with a covering still over his mouth – came and stood next to her, staring at the mess of papers in front of the DI. 'You know what you're doing with this, yes?' Melanie asked, her eyes still fixed to the table.

'Bag and tag,' he said, sounding altogether too cheery. 'I'll collect each sample separately and we'll run them through everything we can. We've already got the box bagged, so we can check that for fingerprints when we're back at the centre as well.'

'Brilliant, thank you,' Melanie said, snapping the latex gloves away from her hands.

'Anything in particular that I'm looking for?'

With a heavy sigh, the DI said, 'A suspect, Zach, you're looking for a suspect.' She turned away, readying herself for a potential confrontation with the grieving parents next door but–

'Mel?' Zach called her back toward the papers. She turned to see him holding one of the many scraps of paper close to his face, as though inspecting it. 'It might not be a suspect, but this looks a lot like your victim.' He handed Melanie a fresh pair of protective gloves, closely followed by a low-resolution image that had been inexpertly printed on regular paper, rather than anything professional or high quality. It took Melanie a hard look to be certain but yes, it was an image of Jenni Grantham, hidden inside this mess of Michael Richards and his victims.

'But why–?' Melanie started but her colleague cut across her.

'Wait, there's something on the back,' Zach said, taking the image back and flipping it.

Melanie read the short bittersweet note, written in what looked to be the same handwriting as the note found on Jenni's body.

Now you see me.

13

DI Melanie Watton had always felt out of place at the Medical Examiner's office; in her years of policing, being around dead bodies had never become a normal part of the job for her. So when she walked into the sterilised space to find George Waller whistling, meanwhile liberating a cadaver of their intestines, something in Melanie's own gut turned over. A gentle heave escaped from behind her paper face mask which pulled George's attention away from the task at hand.

He looked up, mouth still positioned in a perfect O though the whistling sound had ceased, and without a word he looked at the clock pinned to the wall on his left. He frowned at the DI, then, after retrieving his hands from the body in front of him and peeling back his gloves, he crossed the room to meet Melanie. He silently dumped the gloves in a yellow bin and followed that with the plastic spattered apron he'd been wearing.

'I told you to come tomorrow,' he said, staring down the DI.

'I know you did, George, and I'm sorry–'

'No, you're not.' He stepped around her, making his way to his desk that was tucked away in a back corner of the room. 'You're never sorry, DI Watton, it's part of your–'

'Charm?' Melanie offered before George's insult could land and, to her relief, he laughed. George pulled out his chair and sat down heavily in its seat as Melanie closed the distance between them. 'I know you said tomorrow, but what you don't know now you won't know then, and as it stands, we know fuck all about this girl.' George sighed and shot a look at the officer in between her speeches. 'I'm sorry, I know how you feel about cursing but sometimes the occasion calls for it.'

'It's the end of the day, Melanie.' George lifted one pile of papers from his eyeline to make way for another. 'This really couldn't wait until tomorrow?'

'You're still working anyway.' Melanie pointed a thumb to the body behind her.

'It hardly counts.' George followed Melanie's gesture with a point of his own. 'It was a heart attack. I'm just being thorough.'

'Well then, you have the time to discuss something more pressing.'

'Having the time and having the inclination are two different things, officer,' he said, pulling on his reading glasses. A handful of tense seconds followed as George skimmed through the handwritten notes that were laid out in front of him. Having reached the bottom of a page, he looked to Melanie. 'I haven't even written up my results yet, so you're getting the rough and ready version, okay?'

Melanie nodded. 'I'll take any version.'

George ducked down behind his desk for a handful of seconds before reappearing with a stuffed file in tow. He heaved the pile of documents onto the desk and let out a hard puff of air, as though the act had exhausted him. Without a word, he proceeded to skim through the papers at a speed, while Melanie sat patiently awaiting whatever verdict would come.

The two had worked together on a number of cases and Melanie knew that George would have something good for her – or bad, depending on your perspective. But there would certainly be something of use here; there had to be, the officer thought. The first time she had met George, he'd introduced himself as the man with all the answers – she was still in uniform, acting as a glorified security guard for a nightclub killing in the town centre. The case had been a messy one, but it took George all of fifteen minutes to develop a workable theory on the death itself – and he'd turned out to be right too.

'See, all the answers,' he'd told her, tapping the side of his nose and flashing a smile.

The two had been on good terms since and, even though she knew not to rush the man – more than she already had, of course – she felt a sharp pang of irritation for how long he was taking with these latest results.

'George–' Melanie started but he cut her short with a sharp glance over the top of his glasses. He flashed a wide smile at the sheet of paper in front of him before spinning it round for the sheet to face Melanie. The officer scanned the opening paragraph of the paper and quickly discerned that it was an autopsy report from one of the Michael Richards' victims.

Melanie flitted her eyes to the top of the page to locate the specific name: Penny Evans, victim number three. Melanie darted through the details until she reached the end of the report and then looked up to the medical examiner, who appeared much smugger than she felt at that moment.

'We already know there's a Michael Richards link here, George, the problem is not knowing what it is.' She nudged the paper as she spoke. 'You already told me that she'd been killed the same way as these other women.'

'I did, but what I haven't told you yet is that I was wrong.' The smile on George's face didn't quite match his announcement and Melanie felt stumped. 'All of the women that were murdered by Michael Richards were starved of oxygen, you see.' George gestured to the sheet of paper that sat askew between them both. 'That's why the bags were over their heads still; it was his weapon of choice, it's how he actually killed them. But Jenni Grantham is different, was different. The method was all different.' George took on a tone of excitement the further he ventured into his explanation and, while it seemed an inappropriate thing to be excited over, there was something contagious about the idea of a breakthrough. Melanie took on a slight smile herself as she followed George away from the desk and across the room, to the dreaded wall of drawers. Without warning, George opened a door and rolled out the young Jenni Grantham, and Melanie's chipper smile gave way to another involuntary heave. She snapped her head away.

'Jesus, George, shouldn't you warn people before you do that?' she said, still facing away.

'If you don't look, you won't see.'

When Melanie turned back around, George was already gesturing to the young girl's neck. Her skin had been mottled and dirtied the last time Melanie had seen her, but she was clean. If it weren't for the slight abrasions and the blue cobwebs laced over the body, Melanie could almost think the girl was made of porcelain, and that thought saddened her.

'Do you see it?' George asked, pulling Melanie back into the room.

'I see a body, George. What am I meant to see?'

'See this, here?' He pointed to a thickened purple band around the young girl's neck. Melanie nodded and held her eyes fixed on the bruising. 'She wasn't suffocated, she was strangled.' Melanie heard the explanation but struggled to draw a conclusion from it; she shook her head and tried to smooth out an advancing frown. 'One is cutting off air supply, to the nose or mouth, say, with a bag for example.' George explained slowly, as though talking to a child.

'But that's not what happened here?' Melanie looked again at the body.

'She was strangled, not suffocated, which means pressure was directly applied to the neck and therefore the windpipe, blocking her airway for a prolonged period of time until–'

'She stopped breathing.' Melanie finished the explanation as George's findings clicked into place. 'So she was already dead when the bag was placed over her head?'

George held up his hands in a defensive gesture. 'Now, that I can't say. She may have been strangled first, bag placed after; she may have been strangled with the bag already in place. But I wasn't there when the bag was put over her head.' Melanie winced at his frankness. 'My report will read manual strangulation. From the bruising here, it's impossible to draw another conclusion and any ME worth his salt would agree.' He rolled Jenni away, closing the small door firmly behind her. 'Of course, given the evidence for strangulation, it means that she actually wasn't killed in the same way as the Richards' victims. Now, I'm no detective,' he said, leaning back against the wall of closed doors behind him. 'But to me it looks a lot like someone wanted you to think this girl had been suffocated.'

Melanie thought back to the rumpled bag, the tape that had fixed it so firmly in place. 'There's no chance that bruising came from the tape?' the officer asked, throwing in her one last reasonable doubt.

George shook his head. 'When you get my digital recordings on the matter, you'll see photographs that clearly show thumbprints around that neck of hers, plus an x-ray that shows structural damage consistent with strangulation. The tape didn't do it.' George side-stepped Melanie and wandered back to his desk. 'There's no doubt in my mind, Mel, but I'm happy to have a colleague look over the results if it'll set your mind at ease. You already know what this means though, don't you?'

Melanie caught up and seated herself in the chair opposite from him. 'Jesus Christ, George.' She rubbed at her eyes as she spoke, the tiredness of three sleepless nights catching up with her at once. 'The crime scene was staged.'

14

DI Watton, DS Carter, and DC Burton were positioned around a recently emptied desk, their early evidence laid across it. Melanie had shared the latest update regarding the crime scene with her colleagues, much to their collective confusion, but it still hadn't given them much to get started with.

'Why would someone go to so much effort?' Carter asked, his stare fixed on a wide shot of the playing fields that lay on top of a pile of photographs. 'Michael Richards didn't even kill his victims in an impressive way, did he, I mean as killers go…'

His voice trailed off as he noticed his DI's stare, her eyebrow raised to create an unimpressed look.

'I was just saying,' Edd added.

'Don't,' Mel replied, her voice flat.

Chris cleared her throat with a deliberate cough before asking, 'What about the handwriting?'

'What about it?' Melanie snapped back.

'Is there anything of use there, do you think? Can we get some kind of expert in?'

Melanie sighed and glanced at Edd who shrugged.

'Are you prepared to tell the superintendent that we've got

nothing to go on?' Melanie asked but when Chris opened her mouth to proffer an answer, the DI held a flat hand up to halt the DC from speaking. 'It was rhetorical. The handwriting would be useful if we had something to compare it to. We can't compare it to the originals because what would be the point, and we have no other samples to use because that kind of database doesn't exist yet.' Chris looked visibly deflated by the explanation and Melanie felt a pang of guilt at having responded so curtly. 'Under other circumstances, it could work. But I don't see it working here,' she added, trying to soften her rejection.

'Okay, so what will work?' Edd pushed, growing impatient.

'What bright ideas do you have?' Melanie stood as she spoke which left her looking down on her junior officer. Edd physically retreated, leaning back in his seat to put a safe distance between him and the DI. 'We need to talk to Jenni's friends again, I think that's our best move from here on out.' Melanie paced the room with two fingertips pressed to her temples as she spoke. 'We'll need their parents' permission for a formal interview, so I suppose that's the next hurdle. Did the college provide you with any details or does someone need to chase that?' Melanie directed the question to Chris, who flashed a nervous look at Edd before answering.

'We've got their contact details already; Gibbons sent them over, along with the details of one or two other kids who might be useful.'

'We'll pull in the two Jenni was with the night she died, and we can work out from there with one or two others.' Melanie turned to address Edd, who had retreated entirely into a small corner of the room. 'Can you make those phone calls? Try to get through to the parents of the first two, ask them if they'd mind helping us with our enquiries, make it sound as neutral as possible.' Edd nodded by way of a response. 'We've got Read and Fairer going through the CCTV footage from various points around the city, Morris is still working with the tech team. We need something from these college kids,' Melanie said aloud, but Carter felt as though his superior was talking to herself rather than addressing them.

'Chris, can you get onto Gibbons? See if he'll let us talk to these other kids he's mentioned; we should see how the ground lies there.' Melanie waited for a sign of confirmation from her DC before turning to her DS. 'Can you try to get both Patrick and Eleanor in later this afternoon?' she said to Edd.

The DS agreed. 'Any particular time?'

'Straight after college? That'll make it what, four? Four thirty?' Edd and Chris shrugged in unison and Melanie continued. 'Ask one to arrive earlier than the other; book one in for four thirty, if you can, and the other for five thirty. We don't want them to re-write anything while they've still got the chance to.'

'Are we treating them as suspects, boss?' Edd questioned with a hint of scepticism.

'Not necessarily, but we are treating them as the last people to see our victim alive, college kids or not.'

Melanie and Chris stood outside the college, confronted by the same security measures the DC and DS had faced last time. In an impatient gesture, Melanie made a point of looking at her watch and tapping her foot, hoping that there would be a security camera somewhere to see her.

A static crackle pulled the DI's attention back to the intercom. 'Sorry, detectives, I couldn't find Mr Gibbons to verify your appointment, but he's corrected my error. Please come straight through the gates...'

The rest of the instructions trailed off as both women stepped through the still-opening gates without further delay. In the distance, Melanie could already see a man standing in an open doorway, ready to welcome them, she assumed. As instructed by the DI, Chris had only called an hour earlier to request another meeting with a handful of Gibbons' students and the principal had suggested the detectives come down right away. Chris couldn't decide whether he was being suspicious or just especially helpful; either way, she was grateful to have the DI in tow.

'Mr Gibbons?' Mel asked, her hand outstretched in a gesture that seemed to throw the man off guard. Gibbons reciprocated with a slight hesitation, but Melanie tried to hold back on being offended; she didn't have the time for sentimentality. 'I hear you've got some students for us?'

'Indeed, Detective Inspector, indeed. Before we get to that, I wonder if we might step into my office for a moment?' Gibbons suggested, gesturing to the open door behind him.

Melanie leaned round to take a glance before asking, 'Is there something you need to discuss with us beforehand, Mr Gibbons?'

'I thought we might get acquainted,' Gibbons replied, with his picture-perfect smile fixed in place again. But his appearance clearly had the same affect on Melanie as it had done on Chris earlier in the week.

'We're working to quite the timeframe today, Mr Gibbons. Why don't we talk to the kids first and we'll see how the ground lies after?' Melanie said – it was clear she wasn't asking, despite her intonation. Gibbons' smile slipped slightly at the corners but to Melanie's relief, he didn't resist her suggestion. She followed him through the ground floor of the building after this, with Chris two steps behind. All three held a steady silence until Gibbons reached for the door of a classroom, and Melanie held out a hand to halt him. 'Can I verify that neither Patrick Nelson nor Eleanor Gregory are present in the class?'

'Of course, of course, as DC Burton requested,' Gibbons said, looking to Chris.

Gibbons pushed open the door to reveal a small selection of students, most of whom were too preoccupied with their mobile phones to notice that someone had entered the room. With a sharp cough, Gibbons called to attention the seven students who were present and they all turned to assess both Melanie and Chris.

Gibbons addressed the class. 'You are to be honest and helpful toward DI Watton and DC Burton, it goes without saying, I'm sure.' Once his instructions had been delivered, Gibbons stepped aside and took up watch from the doorway, allowing Melanie the spotlight at the front of the room. Chris was perched on a nearby window ledge, her small notepad at the ready.

'I'm sure you're all eager to get back to your classes so I'll try to keep this quick,' the DI said, with a sarcastic edge to her voice. She was grateful to note the smirked responses around the room; it was always a good start to win them over. 'We'd like to know a bit more about Jenni Grantham, and we'd be grateful for any information you can tell us. We don't have pointed questions, but we're wondering what sort of person she was.' Melanie left a deliberate beat of silence before pushing with another query. 'Was she acting differently to usual in the days before her death, did anyone notice?'

There was a longer silence this time as one student looked to another, encouraging each other to be the first to speak.

'No,' came a cracked voice from the back of the room. Melanie glanced around to see another young woman; blonde hair, glasses, her shoulders slightly hunched. 'She didn't act any differently to me, at least, she was still – she was still just kind Jenni.'

There was a murmur of agreement around the room and Melanie's heart sank at the sight of their collective loss.

'You should be talking to Patrick Nelson,' another voice snapped. A young man wearing a bitter expression. 'He was the last to see her, wasn't he?'

Melanie trod carefully. 'What makes you say that?'

'It's common knowledge.' The young man sat up a little straighter as he spoke. 'They were together right before it happened, so why don't you ask him?'

'Alistair, watch your tone,' Gibbons cautioned from the doorway.

'We'll be talking to Patrick in due course,' Melanie said. 'But for now we're curious about anything that other people might know?'

'She and Patrick were quite close in the weeks before her death,' another girl remarked. 'There was nothing to it though; they were just friends, as far as anyone knew.'

Melanie looked from the new speaker to the previous one; this Alistair kid didn't seem convinced by his classmate's explanation.

'Do you know something different, Alistair?' Melanie made a point of using his name.

The young man shot a look at Gibbons before he spoke. 'All I know is that Jenni was alright six months ago. Then she started knocking around with them, and she wasn't alright.'

'What do you mean by alright?' Chris asked but Melanie side stepped Chris's query.

'Who do you mean by them...?'

15

Eleanor Gregory stepped into the investigation room with the awe and wide-eyed excitement of a child visiting Santa's grotto for the first time. DC Chris Burton held the door open as both Eleanor and her mother, an unimpressed-looking Mrs Gregory, trudged in and without instruction, headed toward the table in the centre of the room.

DS Edd Carter followed behind them and gave Chris a sharp nod before taking the door from her and closing it. Both officers seated themselves at the table opposite mother and daughter, and made a show of shuffling through their respective piles of paperwork in dutiful silence. Neither of the officers were especially comfortable with the situation; they were used to staring down middle-aged offenders, not seemingly excited college kids, and as Eleanor continued to gaze around the room in wonder, the officers' discomfort only worsened. Meanwhile, Mrs Gregory huffed and tutted with the impatience of a distant parent; Chris had seen her type before.

'Are you sure that we don't need a solicitor of some description?' Mrs Gregory eventually asked, breaking the deliberate silence.

'We don't think it's necessary at this stage, no, but if you'd be more comfortable–'

'Is this being recorded?' Eleanor cut across Edd before he could complete his generic reply. 'Like, on film or something?' She looked around the room as she spoke, her eyes eventually narrowing on a small red dot in the upper right corner of the space as she focussed in on the electrical equipment. 'A-ha.' Chris turned to verify Eleanor's spot.

'Yes, there's audio and visual equipment in the room, so you'll be recorded,' Chris explained. 'Is that okay for you both?' She glanced at Mrs Gregory as she spoke, but it was really Eleanor's reaction that interested her. The young woman furiously nodded her approval while her mother gave a raised eyebrow and a curt nod. The recording would show that agreement at least, Chris thought, before setting down her paperwork and laying her hands flat on the table top. 'So, for the record, I'm DC Chris Burton and this is my colleague DS Edd Carter.' She gestured to Edd as she spoke. 'You've been asked to come in here today to discuss–'

'So, is he your boss?' Eleanor asked.

'I'm sorry?' Chris replied, thrown by the abruptness of the query.

'In the hierarchy of the department, my rank is senior to DC Burton's, yes,' Edd replied, his tone neutral. 'But, in the context of this interview, you're in safe hands with my colleague taking the lead.' He gave a tight smile that made Eleanor shift uncomfortably in her seat. Ahead of the interview starting, Chris and Edd had decided they would balance each other out; not so much good cop/bad cop as nice adult/unapproachable adult. 'She might respond better to a younger woman. No offence, Edd,' Melanie had advised in the minutes before the interview had started, and both Chris and Edd had taken their boss at her word.

'You think that I can help you?' Eleanor asked, leaning back in her seat.

'We certainly hope so,' Chris replied. She took a tactical pause while she pulled out a white sheet of paper from the pile in front of her; the sheet detailed one or two of the search terms that Jenni had googled in the weeks before her death, meanwhile the others were deliberately redacted. 'We've been looking through Jenni's computer, and we're still looking, but our early searches have found these.' Chris pushed the sheet toward the girl as she spoke, and both mother and daughter leaned forward to read the printed text. 'It looks as though Jenni was doing a lot of research into the Michael Richards murders. Are you familiar with that case yourself?'

'*The* Michael Richards?' Mrs Gregory erupted, 'her interest suddenly caught.

'Yes,' Chris replied. 'You're obviously familiar with the name?'

Mrs Gregory took another look through the list before answering. 'Isn't everyone in this bloody town? I wouldn't expect the girls to be though.' She looked at her daughter questioningly before turning back to Chris. 'Isn't it a bit before their time?'

'I have heard of those killings though,' Eleanor added. 'Jenni had been talking about them.' Eleanor paused to look down the list. 'Friggin' A though, she didn't say she'd been doing this.'

'So, this isn't something you were researching together?' Carter asked and the change in officer seemed to throw Eleanor off balance. She opened her mouth to speak but instead shook her head and looked back down at the list.

'When we saw you at the college, you mentioned that Jenni was dressing as a victim, for Halloween. Do you remember that?' Chris continued.

'A victim?' Mrs Gregory looked taken aback. 'A victim of what?'

'We're hoping your daughter might be able to answer that for us,' Edd replied in a deadpan tone, ignoring the glare of the mother in favour of staring down the daughter. Eleanor refused to make eye contact with him though, instead focusing her attention on Chris.

'I actually didn't say that,' she said. 'Patrick did.'

Chris glanced down as though looking at notes. 'Ah, of course. Was it the first you'd heard of Jenni's plan?'

Eleanor hesitated before answering. 'No. No, it wasn't the first I'd heard of it.'

'So, do you know what she was meant to be a victim of?' Chris pushed.

'No,' Eleanor answered too quickly, her eyes flicking toward the small recording light. 'No, I don't know what she was meant to be a victim of, sorry.' She spoke directly into the camera, her eye contact with the officer broken. The young girl sighed and shifted in her seat before casting a cautious glance at her mother. Eleanor leaned across, closing the gap between them, and whispered something to her mother that neither officer could hear. Edd and Chris shared a concerned look.

'Is there a problem?' Edd asked.

Mrs Gregory looked up before her daughter did. 'Is Patrick Nelson being questioned about this at some point?'

'Can I ask why you're asking that?' Edd's glance shifted between mother and daughter before settling on Eleanor. 'Is there something about Patrick and Jenni that we should know about, Eleanor?'

The young girl sighed and rolled her eyes. 'It was his idea really. You know, we were going to be the killers, and she was going to be the victim.' Eleanor looked from one officer to the other. 'I told you, we were going to be Freddy and Jason, right? You remember that?' she said, craning over as though to look at Chris's notes.

Instinctively, Chris covered the sheet in front of her with a shift of her arm before replying. 'Yes, we remember that.' She threw a look at Edd. 'You're saying it was Patrick's idea?'

Eleanor nodded. 'It was his idea to do like, a three-way Halloween costume. That's why Jenni was dressing as a victim. But,' Eleanor leaned forward to look at Jenni's history of search terms again. 'I don't know what any of this is about though. Like, we didn't have anything to do with that.' Eleanor leaned back and folded her arms across her torso.

'So, is there something Patrick can tell us that you can't?' Edd pushed, again looking between mother and daughter.

Eleanor gave a curt laugh. 'I mean, how could I know that?' She straightened her posture as she spoke. 'I know that he feels really guilty about it though. We weren't even there, and it wasn't even Halloween and like, I've told him it wasn't our fault, obviously. But, you know, the whole costume thing, and Jenni actually, actually going and...' Her sentence petered out, as though she were unsure how to finish it, and at that her mother pushed her seat back from the table and moved to stand.

'Are we finished here?' she asked curtly.

Edd took a glance at the clock on the opposing wall and gave Chris a nod of approval.

'Yes, thank you for your time, both of you,' Chris said, rising from her seat. Eleanor and her mother followed, the three women leaving Edd seated alone at the table. 'I'll take you back through to reception and one of our officers will see you out,' Chris continued.

Edd remained silent while the three headed toward the doorway, only speaking as he heard the door part from the frame. 'We may need to talk to you again, if that won't be a problem.' He didn't turn to address the comment to either daughter or mother particularly, just kept his head down, flicking through papers as though he were disinterested in any answer that either visitor could give. Behind him, Eleanor flashed a questioning look at Chris who nodded in support of Edd's comment, and the young woman pushed her way out of the room, not saying another word.

'Thank you again for your time,' Chris said to Mrs Gregory, depositing her and her daughter back in the reception space before taking a look around the empty chairs of the waiting room. Chris back tracked to the desk sergeant. 'No one else waiting for DS Carter or myself?' she asked, turning around for another look. 'Anyone been in and left?'

'Afraid not. No one since the young lady came in,' the officer replied, pointing towards Eleanor and her mother who were retreating out of the entranceway.

'Shit.'

Chris paced back along the corridor at a determined speed, pushing the door open with such a force that it rebounded off the unsuspecting wall behind it. Edd's head snapped round, his startled expression suggesting that Chris had caught him off guard. 'Problem?' he asked.

'Patrick Nelson hasn't turned up for his interview.'

'Shit.'

16

'**B**ollocks,' DI Melanie Watton snapped into the phone. She leaned back from her uncomfortable makeshift desk and assessed the mess of paperwork in front of her. She had spent the entire day sifting through expired case files relating to Michael Richards, fencing calls from the superintendent at regular intervals, and the DI couldn't help but feel that her and her team were owed a break already, despite the case still being in its early days. On the other end of the line, DS Edd Carter remained silent, giving his boss time to formulate her thoughts before he could cut her off too soon. 'Okay. What was the interview with Eleanor like?'

'She's an interesting kid,' Edd replied.

'He means odd.' Chris raised her voice in the background, half-listening to the DS's conversation with their superior; half-skimming through everything she could find on the Nelson family, which so far wasn't much.

'Interesting how?' Melanie pushed.

'The reason Jenni was dressing as a victim for Halloween was because Eleanor and their missing mate Patrick were dressing as Freddy and Jason, and Jenni was their victim. Not based on anyone in particular, by the sounds of it, just making a three-way costume sort of thing–'

'She wasn't meant to be a Michael Richards victim?' Melanie interrupted.

'Not according to Eleanor, no. She didn't seem to know anything about that part of Jenni's life, also didn't know that Jenni was showing such an interest in the killings either.'

'Someone knew,' Melanie absent-mindedly added, again looking over the mound of paperwork that had built up in front of her over the day. 'I'm still at George Waller's office,' she said, her attention focusing again. She'd spent the day hiding out at Waller's office for fear of the pressure that working at the station would bring, and it helped to have Waller's knowledge of the original murders on hand should she need it. 'It's been a washout of a day though. I may as well try to get something productive done. Can you text me the Nelson address? I'll swing by there on my way home; maybe an in-person chat will be weightier than anything done over the phone.' She exhaled hard and rubbed at her temples where a small wave of pain was starting to roll out beneath her skin; it really had been a long day.

'Do you want one of us to come along?' Edd offered.

'Thanks, but I'll be alright.' She extinguished the call without the courtesy of a goodbye. While she'd appreciate the offer of help on any other day, that day she needed to feel capable of actually getting something done on her own, and an overeager Edd on her coattails was unlikely to help. Melanie stayed seated until the text came through with the address – 24 Marshfield Terrace – and was relieved to see that the Nelson house was only a ten-minute drive away from her own. She collected the mass of papers into something that resembled just the one pile before writing George a quick note – *Thanks again for this. M.* – and leaving the office.

Two minutes later she was in her car, engine humming as the condensation on the windscreen gave way, allowing Melanie a line of sight out of the window. She turned the heat up another degree and pulled away into the busy early evening traffic.

There were lights on inside the Nelson house, which ticked off Melanie's first concern about the prospect of there being no one at home. On the walk from her car to the front door, she straightened out her shirt – creased from a day of desk work – and cleared her throat. She felt for her ID card in her pocket and then pressed a fingertip firmly against the front doorbell. Melanie counted out five seconds before ringing the bell again. 'Alright!' came a curt reply from somewhere inside, and seconds after that the door was snatched open. In the doorway there stood a stout woman; several inches shorter than Melanie, she wore a hairstyle that had been stripped from a 1970s catalogue, but her clothes were modern, albeit plain. Her expression was one of irritation, as though Melanie had interrupted something important, and rather than introduce herself, or even ask Melanie what she wanted, instead the woman merely cocked an eyebrow at the officer, as though this in itself were enough of a greeting.

'I'm DI Melanie Watton. Am I correct in thinking you're Mrs Nelson?'

The woman looked Melanie up and down before answering. 'I am, yes.' Her tone suddenly changed from her earlier abruptness, and the woman straightened up a little as she spoke. 'Is this about the business with the Grantham girl?'

'Ah, yes, it is, so you're aware of our investigations.' Mrs Nelson nodded in response, prompting Melanie to continue. 'You and your son were meant to come down to the station this afternoon to speak to a couple of my officers, so I understand it, only you didn't–'

The woman cut Melanie off with a heavy sigh before turning into the house and shouting: 'Jesus H, love, you didn't call the police?' There was a heavy tread of footsteps rushing down the stairs, ending when an equally stout middle-aged man came to stand alongside Mrs Nelson. 'This is DI,' Mrs Nelson said, but skipped a beat over Melanie's name. 'It's about taking Pat down to the station, but you said you'd call. Didn't you call?'

The man rubbed at the back of his neck and stared firmly at the floor. 'No, no, I suppose I didn't.'

There was another heavy sigh. 'I'm so sorry,' Mrs Nelson said, turning back to face Melanie. 'Apparently I'm married to a bloody idiot.' From behind her, Mr Nelson shrugged in a resigned fashion and retreated into the house. 'Pat came home from college with a terrible stomach and he's been in and out of bed with sickness ever since. My husband,' she said the word like an insult, 'told me that he'd call you to explain while I was tending to Pat, but he obviously found something better to do on his way to the phone.'

'I see,' Melanie replied, trying to sound neutral. 'So, there's no chance of interviewing Patrick this evening, not even a quick chat?'

The woman looked amused. 'I mean, if you're brave enough to go up there...' Melanie held her hands up in a jokey display of defeat. 'Is there something I can be helping you with?'

Melanie grabbed at the opportunity. 'Can you confirm for me whether Jenni Grantham was here on the night of the incident; four nights ago, it would have been.'

Mrs Nelson thought – hard, by the expression on her face – before speaking: 'Yes, she was. They were upstairs playing their music, all three of them were; you know about Ellie, I assume? They were trying out their plans for Halloween or some such. That's all I heard about the night and I haven't been privy to much information since.' She sounded particularly irked by this last admission.

'Patrick isn't saying much about what happened?' Melanie pushed.

'Truth is, he's in a dreadful state. I think he might have been sweet on the girl although he's never told me as much.' Melanie nodded, encouraging the woman to continue. 'Nothing ever happened, not that I know of, but he always had this funny look in his eye whenever he mentioned her. Now when she's mentioned it's a different kind of look altogether.' She sounded sad, sympathy for her son breaking through her words.

'Thank you, Mrs Nelson. This has been helpful,' Melanie said, drawing their encounter to a close. 'When Patrick's feeling better, perhaps you can give us a call and we'll arrange a quick chat with him? There are just one or two things that we need to verify, you understand.' As Melanie spoke, she thumbed at her cardholder to dig out an official business card, which she handed over to the woman in front of her. 'That'll put you straight through to me, if you want to get in touch when you can.'

By the time Melanie was back in her car, the full weight of her exhaustion had settled on her shoulders. How could they not find anything? The victim and her family were squeaky clean on the surface; no one had a bad word to say about any of them, and it seemed that Jenni's friends were in a similar boat. Something about Mrs Nelson's admission stuck in Melanie's side though; the idea that there was more between Patrick and Jenni than anyone knew – or maybe someone did know, or someone found out and objected. Were Patrick and Eleanor meant to be an item?

The thoughts threw themselves around Melanie's head for the short drive home, snapping short when she finally pulled up in front of her house. The case was leaving Melanie stumped, whichever way she looked at it. She eyed the dark house in front of her before restarting the car engine.

These feelings called for a greasy dinner.

17

Melanie stood with her back to the incident room, her narrowed eyes staring down the white evidence board that the team was steadily patchworking together. The space was a mess of photographs – of Jenni, alive and dead, alongside Michael Richards' victims that the young girl may or may not have had some connection to. Melanie shrugged; the Michael Richards link felt like anyone's guess, but there was something about it all that didn't sit right with her. She eyed the question marks that were appearing around Jenni's name: *Victim? Staged? Friends involved?* This last one had been crossed out, and underneath it there was: *Unknown killer? Random attack?* The team was adding their guesses as they thought of them, but there was little in the way of hard evidence helping the case along, and Melanie was already feeling the pinch.

Behind her, the team banded together in the hopes of some kind of progress meeting, but morale was already low. Melanie had filled DC Chris Burton and DS Edd Carter in on the situation with Patrick Nelson, and neither officer looked pleased at having their investigations halted. Meanwhile, DCs Read and Fairer were already putting their heads together to confer over a bare-looking sheet of paper that Read was holding in a determined grip.

'Got something for us?' Melanie asked, nodding towards Read's sheet.

The officer sighed. 'I bloody wish.'

'It's a notice from forensics, no official results yet,' Fairer explained.

'Maybe if they weren't busy putting everything in writing, they'd have time to do their jobs,' Read added, folding the paper in half and scoring it with his thumbnail; the movement looked surprisingly aggressive on him. 'What are they playing at over there; can't we put a rush on this sort of thing?'

'There is a rush on,' Melanie said, perching on the table next to the evidence board. 'They're covering themselves that's all, lads, making sure they've got a logged timeline in place for whatever happens next.' Fairer didn't look convinced by the explanation but he let the conversation slide all the same; he'd learnt that when it came to his boss's word, there wasn't usually much room to dispute it. 'So nothing on forensics?' Melanie asked.

'They've found fibres on Jenni's clothes that they're trying to build up some kind of a profile for; some look like they've come from the college wear. Apparently one of the tech blokes has a kid at the place and he'd know the colour a mile off. But some of the samples look like they've come from elsewhere. Where elsewhere is...'

'Remains to be seen?' Melanie finished Read's explanation and he nodded. 'How certain are they that some of the fibres are college wear?'

'Certain enough to have told us, which I suppose counts for something,' Read guessed.

'Okay.' Melanie turned to write on the board. 'The college doesn't have a strict uniform policy, generally, but they do have hoodies, in the college colour, with emblems stitched to them. So, presumably, it's either the hoodie,' she paused to write this word on the board, 'or it's the emblem.' She wrote this word and followed both with a question mark before circling the words and drawing a line stretched out from them. She turned to address the team again. 'The question is, why would she have been wearing college wear on the day that she died; was there an event, a match, an anything? From there, how did they come into contact with her Halloween clothes; are we assuming this contact is with the clothes from the scene? In which case, are we assuming that they're Eleanor's?'

There were so many questions, but before anyone could guess at an answer, the door to the incident room slammed open with a force that made the officers snap their attention around to it. DC Lucy Morris stood there, panting air back into her chest as though she'd run a marathon to get there.

'High speed pursuit?' Fairer asked and there was a low chuckle around the room.

'We've found her,' Morris huffed out. 'We've found Jenni, on CCTV.'

Melanie and her team crowded around the collection of screens that made up Morris's makeshift office. She'd been watching camera reel after camera reel for two days, and the team being in here felt like an intrusion on her personal space. But the young officer shook off the discomfort at having company around her and clicked through the video files that were lined up on her desktop. She clicked one, prompting a saturated image to load onto the screen; in one edge of the frame there was a corner shop just barely visible.

'So, we're angled just above the entrance to this shop here,' Morris explained, situating the team in the location on screen. 'It's off Southampton Street with owners who were kind enough to volunteer their recordings for the last week when I called them.' With a click, the film started rolling, and just seconds later, Jenni Grantham appeared on screen. 'There's our girl,' Morris said, pausing the clip.

'Our girl, wearing a college hoodie,' Carter highlighted.

'Wait, did you say Southampton Street?' Melanie asked.

Morris spun around in her seat to face her boss. 'I did. I wondered when one of you would notice.' She shot a playful look at the rest of the team; finding a lead had finally given the young officer a confident streak. 'I wasn't getting anywhere going through the direct roads from Patrick Nelson's house to Jenni's house, and frankly, there aren't that many alternative routes she could have taken. There were a lot out of her way that she could have taken though, and she did.' She turned to pull up another video file. This one showed Jenni again walking down a small strip of independent shops. 'This is about ten minutes on from the Southampton Street shot, which fits with how long it would have taken her to walk there.'

'All of those files you've got,' Edd said, pointing toward the screen. 'They're all Jenni?'

Lucy nodded. 'They're all Jenni.' Lucy back-clicked from the still image currently occupying the screen and, laying a fingertip on the first image icon she'd opened, she said, 'From Southampton Street, to Indie Row, to Baker Walk, all the way through to...' Lucy moved about between icons as she spoke, eventually pausing to click open the penultimate icon showing at the bottom of her screen. 'Security shots from outside The Black Hound public house.'

Jenni walked in from the top of the screen with a man trailing behind her, but it was clear that they weren't together. The team watched on in a tense silence as Jenni turned to speak to the man, whatever she had said prompting him to grab her arm, before Jenni pulled away and walked out of shot.

'Is that all we have?' Melanie snapped, her tone sharp with what sounded like impatience.

Again, Lucy back-clicked and dropped her cursor onto the final icon. 'The Black Hound is a big place, so they've got several security cameras installed, luckily for us. But this is the last one that shows anything of Jenni.'

Jenni tumbled into view as though she had been gently pushed before turning around and saying something to someone off-screen. A second later, the same man from before joined her in the frame. The team didn't need an audio accompaniment to see that the pair were arguing; Jenni appeared to be doing the majority of the shouting though, her young face furious, her arms gesturing wildly. The man standing opposite her seemed, if anything, somewhat amused. He leaned toward her as though to grab her shoulders and Jenni backstepped, a warning index finger extended as though she were reprimanding a child. Mere seconds passed before Jenni stepped out of the frame; the man reached out then and pulled her back but with a tug of the shoulders, Jenni's hoodie slipped away from her and she'd gone.

Lucy hit pause, allowing the unknown man's face to hover on the screen.

'That's the last we see of her?' Burton asked, breaking her concentration on the screen for the first time since this slideshow had started. Lucy nodded confirmation. 'Anything more from him?' Chris nodded toward the screen.

'I'm out of footage. He might appear elsewhere, but we'll have to go digging to find him.'

'I don't want footage,' Melanie announced. She leaned over the desk to closer inspect the man on the screen. 'I want the real thing.'

18

R obert and Evie Grantham sat side by side on their sofa with DI Melanie Watton and DS Edd Carter perched on the seats opposite them. The group waited quietly while DC Ian Dixon, the Family Liaison Officer, clinked about in the kitchen, making tea and coffee as required. Melanie shared an awkward beat of eye contact with Robert, who then lowered his eyes to scrutinise the file that Melanie was holding.

'Can you not just tell us what all this is about?' Robert asked, stern, almost business-like. Melanie opened her mouth to respond but was cut short by the arrival of Dixon, who backed into the living room door and turned to reveal a tray full of steaming cups.

'Who was tea and who was coffee?' he asked the room, before distributing the drinks.

'Mr Grantham.' Melanie sat forward to lessen the distance between her and the couple. 'We've found some footage of Jenni on various CCTV feeds from the evening that she was attacked.' Evie Grantham took a sharp intake of breath which forced a pause from Melanie, but the officer knew she needed to press on. 'In the final minutes of footage, Jenni appears with an unknown male outside a local public house. We will be putting out a call for information to try to get the man to come forward, but we were wondering whether you might be able to look at an image of the individual in question to see whether you recognise him at all?'

'Did he hurt her? Is that what you're thinking? Did this man hurt her?' Evie Grantham asked with urgency, sitting forward in her seat, pulling away from her husband who looked physically pained by his wife's reaction.

'Evie,' he said, as though to settle her. She threw a look back at him, but Melanie couldn't quite spot the woman's expression; then Evie was looking forward again, braced to catch Melanie's answer. 'You said the photograph was taken outside of a public house; a pub in town you mean, that's where Jenni was seen?'

'That's where we've found footage of her, yes.'

The parents shared a glance. 'What the bloody hell would she have been doing there?' Evie snapped, as though Melanie could, should, be able to explain their daughter's actions.

'We picked her up on a number of routes through the town centre on the evening of the attack.' Melanie tried to soften her tone, aware of the blow she was delivering. 'We're hoping that by talking to this man, we might be able to get more of an idea of where she'd been, or where she was going.' Melanie thumbed the file open to retrieve the picture as she spoke.

'It's a still image that we've pulled from the footage we found,' Carter explained. 'The quality might not be the best,' he said as his senior handed over the sheet. 'But our team are working to get a clearer image together, for the press release.'

Robert took the extended sheet of paper from Melanie and eyed the pixelated image. It showed a man, his arms outstretched, and in one hand there was an item of clothing. Robert brought the image closer to inspect it in more detail, but he still couldn't work out what the clothing was. From the expression on the pictured man's face, he was mid-speech; his mouth moulded into a perfect O. Robert scrutinised the copy for a second longer before shaking his head lightly and passing it to his wife, who had been craning to see the image over her husband's shoulder.

She took the sheet eagerly, as though snatching for a prize, and stared at it with a fierce intensity. Melanie and Edd shared a questioning look but neither were prepared to rush through this moment; it was the first potential break in the case, and that would be a lot for any grieved parents to process.

Dixon stood just inside the doorway, on call should anyone need him. The young FLO caught Edd's eye and nodded, to gesture out of the room, before Dixon excused himself. Seconds later, Carter followed. When Carter arrived in the kitchen, Dixon quietly closed the door and turned to face his colleague.

'Where are we at?' he asked.

Carter shrugged and rubbed at the back of his neck. 'This is the first major break.' He sighed. 'Potentially major break,' he corrected himself. 'DC Morris, back at the station, had been wading through security footage for the best part of two days before she found this, and she only found this because she expanded her search to include–'

Melanie pushed open the kitchen door, cutting Edd off mid-explanation. Without a word, she nodded him back into the living room and retreated there herself. When both officers were seated in their previous positions, Melanie said, 'So, to fill in my colleague, neither of you recognise the man in this image?'

Robert shook his head. 'He doesn't look like anyone we know, I don't think?' He turned to his wife for verification and she nodded, solemnly, in agreement. 'But you think he's involved somehow, with our girl?'

'That's what we're hoping to find out.' Melanie slipped away the photograph. 'The next steps will be to release this image to the press in the hope that we might be able to track down the man. He's a person of interest, at the moment; we don't have enough information about his involvement to go as far as calling him a suspect,' she added, pre-empting what the couple's next query would be. 'But tracking him down will be a step in the right direction, of that much we're certain.'

The Granthams absent-mindedly nodded along in time with Melanie's delivery, but their faces remained tortured, on the brink of tears. 'While we're here we do have one question, if you don't mind. Do you happen to know where Jenni's college hoodie would be, the one showing the institute's emblem?' It was clear what the man was holding in that final shot, but what wasn't clear was what happened in the seconds after when the man had disappeared from the frame again. Did he keep Jenni's hoodie; was it Jenni's hoodie at all, or someone else's? Melanie knew that she must look everywhere for a link, no loose thread too small...

Robert looked to his wife who, without word, rose from her seat and exited the room. There was the sound of footsteps thudding upstairs, arriving in a room directly above the living room by the sounds of it, and then shuffling. Melanie imagined drawers being opened, clothes being moved, perhaps even things being overturned.

When Evie Grantham emerged again, she looked dishevelled, as though she'd been searching upstairs for hours rather than mere minutes.

'It isn't there,' she announced, her eyes fixed firmly on the detectives. 'It isn't in her room, I don't think, not that I can find. Do you have it?' She spoke directly to Melanie, her tone more frantic than it had been seconds earlier.

'It's an item of interest at the moment,' Melanie said. 'Do you happen to remember whether her name was sewn into the hoodie, Evie, was that something that she did?' Melanie tried to lower her voice, as though addressing a startled child, but it was clear that Evie Grantham wasn't listening. Melanie stood and crossed the space toward the grieving mother who hadn't ventured into the room entirely, but instead remained hovering in the doorway. Melanie lowered herself into Evie's eyeline and rested a hand on her shoulder. 'We will find out what happened to her, I promise you that.'

At this, a small tumbling of tears erupted from Evie Grantham's eyes and her body hunched over in a gesture that suggested more tears were coming. Taking a cue, Dixon appeared behind the woman in an instant, setting an arm around her and guiding her past Melanie and back to the sofa, to her waiting husband.

Carter stood and joined his superior at the door.

'We'll be releasing this image as soon as we can,' Melanie said, 'with accompanying details of where and when it was captured. You might find that people try to contact you directly about this...' Her sentence faded out as Dixon shot her a soft smile.

'I'll handle that side of things,' he said, reassuring his superior.

'Thank you, both,' Melanie said weakly. Robert acknowledged her comment with a brief nod, but Evie remained passive, her tears still falling at a speed. 'We'll see ourselves out and we'll be in touch with further details,' Melanie finished, her junior officer already halfway down the hallway to the front door. Edd eased the door open and slipped out first. Melanie followed, closing the door quietly behind her before expelling a deep sigh, her breath spilling out of her into the cold outdoors, forming a small cloud.

'You driving us back?' Edd asked and Melanie silently threw the keys at him, heading toward the passenger seat. Both officers climbed into the vehicle and Edd waited until the engine was humming before initiating another conversation. 'What's going on, boss?'

Melanie sighed. 'I can't make sense of it. Where was she going, Edd? Why was she even there?' She rubbed at her temples as she spoke, kneading at the beginnings of a sharp pain in her head. 'On the surface, she was a normal kid. Behind the scenes, she was researching killers, playing victim, walking around town at all hours. What are we meant to make of that?'

Edd clicked the heating up a notch and eased the car away from the curb. 'We don't make anything of it. We keep looking and we make something of what we've got. We'll get there, Mel, we always do.'

Melanie gave him a tight smile in response to his enthusiasm and while she wanted – truly wanted – to believe in Carter's optimism, there was something about this entire case that was already making her doubt herself.

19

DI Melanie Watton was seated at a long table. To her left, sat DS Edd Carter and to her right, DC Chris Burton, both officers' expressions set with stern confidence in the face of the horde of press in front of them. With the permission of Superintendent Beverley Archer, Melanie had arranged for a press conference of sorts, to allow her and her team to formally release the image and accompanying footage of the man who had been with Jenni Grantham on the night of her death.

The press room was packed with familiar and new faces, and Melanie felt an early twist of nerves in her stomach; she'd fenced questions from some of the journalists in this room before, and she knew that they weren't likely to go easy. She glanced toward Burton who was staring directly into the crowd, making eye contact with no one person but rather moving from individual to individual, as though sizing up her threats.

Melanie shifted her glance to Carter, who was looking through the notes in front of him like a student cramming in last minute revision. The sight of both colleagues was enough to put Melanie's mind at ease and, with a click of a button, the television screen alongside the panel changed from a police emblem into a still CCTV shot, and the room instantly fell silent.

Melanie cleared her throat. 'We have discovered CCTV footage of Jenni Grantham from the night that she was murdered. The full clip, which will be available shortly, shows Jenni with an unknown male outside The Black Hound public house in the centre of town.' Melanie paused to show the clip of Jenni conversing with the man in question, ahead of her abruptly exiting the shot, leaving her hoodie in the hands of the man left behind. 'We have been able to isolate a still image of the man featured in this footage.' Melanie clicked to move from the video footage to a still shot. 'If this man is still in the area, we'd very much like to talk to him in relation to the Jenni Grantham case. We hasten to add that at this time the man is merely a person of interest, who we would very much like to talk to.' Melanie clicked again to shut the screen down. 'My colleagues and I are open to questions relating to the case, within reason, if there's anything that anyone wants or feels the need to ask.'

A wave of hands appeared around the room; there were at least eight questions waiting to be launched at the panel already. Edd shot Melanie a quick look and a supportive smile before turning back to face their audience.

'Yes.' Melanie pointed to a man in his mid-thirties sitting in the front row.

'This man that you're looking for, are you treating him as a suspect?'

'No, as I've clearly stated, the man is just a person of interest at this present time, and we'd like to speak to him in relation to Jenni's whereabouts and state of mind when he saw her. Any information he has could be integral to the next steps we take with the case.' Melanie leaned forward, holding steady eye contact with her questioner, but no sooner had she finished her reply than another question was fired, unprompted and without permission, from somewhere at the back of the room.

'And is that because you're drawing blank after blank with the case currently?'

Burton's head snapped in the direction of the question; the new voice was a distinctive one. Heather Shawly worked at The Sun and Star newspaper, where she'd been their crime correspondent for longer than anyone cared to mention. She stood tall at the back of the room, her blonde hair perfectly tamed to curl up in a bounce at the ends. Her make-up looked as though someone had been paid to do it for her; meanwhile her clothes looked like she should be in front of a camera rather than in a police briefing room.

'We're hardly drawing blank after blank,' Melanie said but Heather cut across her.

'This is the first official statement that you've been able to make though, is it not?' Heather pushed, her notepad at the ready although she hardly seemed inclined to write anything down; the woman was clearly looking for an argument – or a misplaced comment from Melanie to quote from, at least. Melanie couldn't help but wonder whether that argumentative streak was what made Heather so successful.

'We're not in the business of handing out details of ongoing investigations unless there's a need for it,' Carter jumped in to defend his boss, although Melanie wished that he wouldn't.

Heather gave a head tilt and a patronising smile. 'But you're in the business of asking the public for their help with a murder investigation?'

'You're a crime correspondent, Ms Shawly, I'm certain that you've seen this procedure before,' Melanie snapped, her tone curt and dismissive. 'As for us drawing blank after blank, we know the where, the how, and even, partially, the why.' Melanie was bluffing, but she was making a good show of it. 'Unfortunately, as is often the case with murder investigations, we're lacking the who. Insofar as asking the public for help, the police aren't in the business of knowing every single person in any given town, so yes, if anyone does know the man in question, we'd like to hear from them; and yes, in the interest of making this town safe again, we are looking to the public for any information they might have.' Melanie inhaled sharply, as though attempting to suck the words back in, but they were out there – worse still, the outburst was on record. The DI quickly consoled herself – she hadn't said anything untrue, after all – but she also dropped her head and avoided eye contact with the infamous Heather, for fear that this conversation might continue.

'Are there any further questions?' Burton asked. Her intervention provided the room with a quick recovery after the recent tension.

A young woman standing close to Heather jumped in, unprompted. 'So, are you saying that the town currently isn't safe?' she asked, alluding to Melanie's earlier comment.

'We're not looking to put the fear of God into anyone,' Chris said, her tone deliberately level and calm in a bid to counteract Melanie's outburst. 'We don't have reason to believe that a similar incident will take place again, nor do we have any reason to believe that the town is under immediate threat of...' Chris petered out, searching for the right word. 'Under immediate threat from the person behind Jenni's murder,' she finished. It was a clumsy close, but it would have to do.

'So, really, you're saying that there's a murderer out there who you know nothing about, but we probably shouldn't worry about it?' Heather spoke over a young journalist in the centre of the room, who was a mere handful of words into his question when the senior reporter stepped over him to voice her point. When Chris nor her colleagues offered an answer, Heather pushed again. 'Is that right, DC Burton, or am I misunderstanding?'

Chris froze; it was one thing to be involved in a murder investigation, but another thing entirely to be singled out like this, to be publicly accountable. Melanie sensed Chris's tension and shot her colleague what was intended to be a reassuring look before turning to address the PC standing at the back of the room: 'Can you escort Ms Shawly out, please?'

Heather let out a harsh laugh than made Chris wince. 'Thank you, officer, but I'll see myself out. I think I've got enough anyway,' she said, addressing the words not to the officer standing next to her but to Melanie herself, who was staring down the journalist with a hard glare.

Melanie's watchful eyes followed the woman out of the room and when the door was firmly closed, with a near-physical weight lifted from her shoulders, Melanie started afresh. 'Now, if there are any further questions about the case...'

20

D S Edd Carter cracked open a can of Diet Coke and lifted his feet to rest on the coffee table. He took three long swigs of the drink, followed by a satisfied 'Ahh' that would have been funny, had there been anyone around to appreciate it. It was well after Emily's bedtime and she was, once again, spending the night at Edd's mother's house – but he still couldn't bring himself to drink anything stronger than a low sugar soft drink, lest he be called out in the middle of the night for a parenting emergency. For company, rather than any real interest, Edd grabbed the remote control and flicked on the television and, in a strange twist, he was greeted by the sight of his own face. Solemn and subdued, he found himself facing down with his earlier self, sitting inside the press room at the station. There was a clip of Melanie talking, bulbs flashing, and the footage cut just before past-Edd spoke.

'Thank God for that,' Edd muttered before taking another sip.

The footage was replaced by the CCTV clip that the police had officially released to the public. There were pleas being made left, right, and centre, and even one or two nationals were getting in on the story it seemed. Edd – and the rest of his team, he knew – were desperate for a break, and he hoped that this exposure would bring about the luck that they needed. However, this quick flicker of optimism gave way to annoyance when the CCTV footage ended, only to be replaced with a shot of Heather Shawly sitting inside a well-lit newsroom.

'And is that because you're drawing blank after–' Edd hit the off button and plunged the woman into silence. But the new quiet of the television set coincided with the loud bang of Edd's front door being closed in the hallway. He sat rigid on the sofa and stared toward the open doorway leading into the living room. It wasn't the prospect of an intruder that unnerved him; it was the fact that only one other person had a door key...

Trish came into view in the doorway. Angling herself to look directly at Edd, she met his eye contact without a flicker of nerve or embarrassment – two things that Edd very much thought his wife should be feeling. Without a word, he looked her over and noted one or two slight differences: her hair was a darker shade of blonde, her jeans a tighter fit than usual, her general posture ever so slightly more relaxed. Although if Edd had run away from his responsibilities without so much as a word of warning to anyone, he imagined he'd feel quite relaxed too. She pressed her back against the doorframe, as though propping herself, and opened her mouth to speak before just as quickly changing her mind. The silence swelled between them until Edd finally cracked. 'You've got a nerve, you know?' he said, standing from his spot on the sofa. 'You've also got some explaining to do.'

Trish exhaled hard. 'Where's Emily?'

'With her grandparents.'

'Why isn't she here?' Trish demanded, a note of irritation in her voice.

'There's a long and short answer to that, which would you like?' Edd matched her tone and took two steps forward, closing the gap between them slightly. 'She's there because I'm working twelve-hour days on a murder investigation and my wife, Emily's mother,' he paused here to point at Trish, 'that's the part that you're supposed to play, decided to up and leave us both without word or explanation. So yes, Mother Duck, I'm afraid she's been having the odd night with her grandparents over the last two weeks. Dare I ask where you've been having the odd night?' Edd accompanied the question with a raised eyebrow but as Trish opened her mouth to offer a response, he held up a hand to pause her. 'Honestly, Trish, I don't even want to know.'

Edd pushed past her and headed toward the kitchen. Without invitation, Trish followed. He grabbed the kettle and took it to the sink to fill with water, meanwhile Trish ventured fully into the room and sat down at the centre table. When Edd set the kettle to boil, he turned around to find his wife staring at him, her eyes shining with the beginnings of tears, and he had to make some effort to swallow down an outburst; the rage he felt toward her in that moment was simmering just beneath the surface.

Trish lowered her head and spoke toward the table. 'I'm so sorry, Edd.'

He sighed. 'I figured that much.' He pulled out a chair and sat down opposite her. In the background, the kettle caused a small shudder through the work surface as it came to a boil and Edd caught his wife's eye. 'You can make the first brew; I suppose we're in for a long night.'

Trish crossed the kitchen to the work surface and took Edd's favourite cup down from their steel mug tree. He tried hard not to feel a pang of almost-love for her, but Edd knew already that these were going to be difficult feelings to shake...

It was nearly eight the following morning when Edd pushed

through the door into the incident room and already the space was alive and buzzing. DI Melanie Watton's office door was closed and, through the open slats of her blinds, Edd could see DCs Fairer and Read standing inside talking to her. He seated himself at his desk and turned on his aging desktop computer, resting his head gently in his hands while he waited for the machine to kick into life. Before the whirring had come to a halt, Edd was stirred by the brush of a cardboard cup being placed on his desk. DC Chris Burton looked down at him, a sympathetic smile on her face:

'Double shots, you look like you need it.' She nodded to the cup before crossing to her own desk and taking a seat.

'Anyone ever tell you that you're an angel?' Edd asked, before removing the plastic lid from the drink and blowing gently against the liquid inside. 'Jesus, just the smell of it is doing the trick.' Edd continued to blow as he turned back to his monitor and typed in his log-in details.

'Late night?' Chris asked.

Edd gave a curt laugh. 'I didn't get much sleep, to be honest.'

'Too much information, Carter.'

'I should be so lucky,' Edd replied, staring at his screen for fear that his face might give away the discomfort he was feeling. It had been a sleepless night of harsh conversations and shocking revelations that had left Edd feeling like he was married to a stranger. Discussing that feeling with someone else – even Chris – was still a little too much to bear.

Melanie's door opened from somewhere behind the pair of officers and the DI came storming out, quickly followed by the DCs with whom she'd been locked in conversation. Carter had never been so grateful for one of his boss's sudden interruptions. Melanie crossed the office space toward the white evidence board at the back of the room and, sectioning off a new square in the centre of the board, she turned to address the room at large.

'Can you shift yourselves over. We've got news worth sharing here.' She held a stern gaze while her team rearranged themselves, shuffling one by one from their desks until they were positioned around the board. Melanie turned back to the white space and wrote *Forensics* at the top of the box before nodding to DC Fairer, who promptly joined her at the front of the space. 'Fairer and Read have been dealing with forensics and at long last we have news, game-changing news, I'd say, so perk up your ears.' She stepped to one side, allowing her junior to take the floor.

Fairer marked a bullet point on the board and next to it wrote *Fibres*. 'Forensics found fibres on Jenni's clothing, which they told us about from the off, but they've now been able to match some of those fibres in a little more detail. As suspected, there's a partial match between some of them and the college hoodies that most of the students own. But there are also transferred fibres that don't match anything that Jenni was wearing. There's a chance these came from Eleanor or Patrick, as they were both with her on the evening of the attack. We'll be arranging for their clothes from that night to be sent to forensics shortly. God willing they've still got them.' Fairer swapped a grieved glance with Melanie, who nodded for him to continue. He listed a second bullet point and wrote *DNA*.

'The real game changer is that they've managed to get a clear DNA sample from Jenni, or, more specifically, from the bag that was secured around Jenni's neck.' Fairer paused to let the details sink in, while his colleagues swapped looks that were somewhere between hopeful and inquisitive. 'The shitter is that the DNA they've found isn't listed in the system.'

'So, we're talking first-timer?' DC Lucy Morris piped up from the back of the crowd.

'Or first time caught,' Melanie said, her tone deadpan.

Carter cleared his throat. 'Do you think it's likely, that it's a first-timer, I mean?'

Melanie frowned before admitting, 'We won't know until we catch him.' She turned back toward Fairer then, nodding for him to continue with his address.

'Obviously, without the individual being listed in the system, we're limited on what we know about them. So far, we've been able to determine that the DNA is male, and that's about as detailed as it's likely to get. There are more tests that they can run but, frankly, they've got better things to be doing with their time.' Fairer shrugged.

Burton huffed out a derogatory snort. 'Like what?'

'Like trying to work out the details of the second DNA donor that left traces on Jenni's body,' Melanie announced from beside the board. Fairer shot her a pained look, clearly disappointed that he'd been robbed of his big reveal. 'You were taking too long,' she said, easing the board pen from his hand and resuming her position centre stage to address her team. There was a sheet of silence sitting over the room as each individual chewed over the information. Melanie allowed them a moment before continuing. 'They've found traces of a second individual; these samples are much smaller, and it took a fair bit of hunting to find them at all. Subsequently, it'll take some work to draw any conclusions from them.'

'But they're placing some significance on them all the same?' Chris pushed.

'The DNA was underneath Jenni's fingernails, but it looks as though someone tried to remove it, which is what's disturbed the sample so much. All they can say for certain at the moment is that it's different to the DNA that was left on the bag.'

'Male, female?' Edd asked.

'Anyone's guess,' Fairer answered before Melanie could.

'So, we've got fibres, clothing to check, DNA to match. We have leads, right? Surely this is a good thing,' Edd said, taking on a tone of optimism that didn't suit his tired expression.

'Exciting as all of that is, we've got another possibility to consider here,' Melanie said, turning to write on the board behind her. When she stepped away, she revealed her latest addition to the evidence board, written in beneath DC Fairer's earlier points.

Two killers?

21

Melanie couldn't sleep. The reveal of a DNA breakthrough was brilliant, but it still didn't give them much to go on. The fact that a second person was at least present, but also possibly involved, complicated matters in terms of not only who they were looking for, but how they'd track down two people when they'd been struggling to track down one. Despite it being nearly the weekend, and her team needing a rest, Melanie had ordered a first-thing meeting with her detectives to discuss the latest discoveries in more detail. There had been a groan around the room at the thought of arriving early on a Saturday, so the DI had promised breakfast to soften the blow. They were a good team, she thought, they would be there no matter what time she needed them.

With a fresh non-alcoholic beer in hand, she wandered back into her dining room where various case files were spread out across the table. There were pictures of victims – old and recent – transcripts of interviews, an overhaul of everything that they'd found on Jenni's computer to date and, alarmingly, they were still finding things there too. Melanie glanced down the growing list of search terms and shook her head; freedom and trust were two valuable things, but it looked as though Jenni hadn't been ready for either.

It had become a nightly practice for Melanie to walk into this room – to her home-from-work evidence board – and stare down everything that they had so far. For the last two nights, she had believed that something, at some point, would jump out at her, but so far there had been no obvious breakthroughs. With a heavy sigh, she grabbed her laptop from the far end of the table and took a seat. The machine was ancient, especially compared to the standard of computer that Melanie usually used at work. The laptop had hardly whirred into life when the sound of the DI's phone cut through the silence of the house, calling her into the hallway. She pulled her phone from her coat pocket and glanced at the screen – DS Carter – ahead of hitting the answer button.

'News?' she said, cutting their formalities.

'They've found him, the bloke from the camera footage,' Edd announced, sounding out of breath. 'Returned to the scene of the crime, of sorts, someone called the station to say that the bloke we were looking for was drinking at The Black Hound. Uniform took it upon themselves to check it out and he was sitting there boozing, brass bollocks and all.'

For the first time since this mess had started, Melanie felt a stab of luck.

'Have they got him at the station?' she asked, tugging on her coat.

'He's in the drunk tank for the night by the looks of him.'

'I'm coming down anyway. I want to see this one for myself.'

Within five minutes, Melanie was out the door and powering through the quiet streets to get to the station. She arrived in half the time it would have normally taken her, but Edd said nothing about the speed of her arrival when he watched her stroll through the station doors just fifteen minutes after them having finished their call. On spotting her junior, Melanie thought that he looked about as tired as she felt, but it didn't seem right to comment on it.

'Were you busy?' Edd said in greeting.

'With what?' She laughed. 'Were you?'

Edd had walked out on another difficult conversation with Trish; the 'Can I come home?' conversation that had been somewhat inevitable since she'd arrived back in the city. The couple had been in the depths of making a decision that would be best for their whole family – a phrase that Trish had used without any embarrassment or irony – when the station's private number had flashed across Edd's phone, alerting him to one new emergency or another. The DS had wasted no time. Not only had he excused himself from the house, but he'd seen Trish out too, and he'd raced to work with an urgency that matched Melanie's.

'Friday night, boss, I'm never busy,' Edd said, gesturing towards a hidden corridor as he spoke. Melanie stepped before him and treaded the path down to the drunk cell at the bottom of the walkway. The so-called drunk tank – or, more accurately, drunk tanks – were also the cells furthest away from the sergeant's desk; a strategic decision that Melanie thought the uniforms were wise for having made.

'What sort of state is he in?' she asked Edd, who was a mere three steps behind her.

'Not disorderly, but nowhere near sober enough for us to question him.' Both officers drew to a halt outside the bolted cell door. 'Apparently the landlord recognised him from the news report days ago but didn't want to say anything until he'd got the man in hands.'

Melanie flashed a smile. 'Citizen's glory?'

'Something like that, I should think.'

Edd pulled down the observation shield and stepped to the side to allow his superior access.

Melanie came level with the open space and saw their man, flat on his back on the hardened bench, his mouth wide open and his eyes firmly shut with sleep. For someone who'd been collared in relation to a murder investigation, the man certainly wasn't worried enough to kick up a fuss over the situation – that, or he was more drunk than anyone had realised. Even from this angle, Melanie could recognise him from the pixelated image on the security feed. She'd spent so much time studying that shot, she thought she would recognise the man anywhere. But seeing him so close gave her a stirring of something in her gut; she had to believe that this was a strong step forward for the case.

She closed the metal grid back up and turned to Edd. 'Sight for sore eyes, isn't he.'

Edd laughed. 'He was when they brought him in, to be fair.' Both officers turned to tread their way back up the corridor. 'So, questioning him first thing?'

Melanie considered this. 'Lunchtime, I think.'

'You want him to get over his hangover first?'

'No, I want him to start worrying.'

The officers held a comfortable silence while they backstepped their way to the front desk. For a Friday night, everywhere seemed suspiciously quiet; although Melanie suspected that would change in the next hour or two. She glanced at her watch – 11:30pm – and realised it was a bit too early in the evening for the real trouble anyway.

'Are you okay to be here first thing?' she asked, coming to a stop in front of the main exit. 'I don't know how childcare is at the moment.' She spotted a twinge of something in Edd's expression that made her wish she hadn't asked. 'I don't mean to speak out of turn. Something is obviously going on, Carter, but you're under no obligation to tell me what. I just need to know whether you're okay for the field tomorrow.' She softened the comment with a smile but tried to keep her tone all business.

'I'll be here, bright and early, but I'm still expecting a buttie,' he replied.

'Deal. Are you heading out?'

'Soon, there's something I need to grab from upstairs.'

'I can wait?'

'No, no, you're good, boss.'

Melanie felt as though she'd missed something, but after her earlier comment she thought it would be too much to push again. She turned to go but one last query pulled her back. 'I should have asked earlier but it'll niggle if I don't ask now. Why did they call you, not me?'

Edd's mouth cracked into a smile followed by a barely contained laugh. 'It turns out it was our honourable PC Shields who dragged his partner down to the pub to check out the report tonight.'

Melanie thought hard to tie the name to something. 'The kid with the evidence boxes?'

'Yep, the kid with the evidence boxes.' Edd paused to swallow another bubble of laughter. 'Turns out he's a...' he hesitated, as though choosing his words carefully, but he admitted a quick defeat: 'Ah, fuck it, he's scared of you. That's why he called me, not you, because he was too nervous to speak to you.'

'Hm.' Melanie considered this for a minute before matching her partner's apparent amusement. 'Good,' she said, and followed it with a wink before she stepped out of the open doors and into the frosted evening.

22

DI Melanie Watton hit the snooze button on her alarm clock and stared at the ceiling. She hadn't fallen asleep until two in the morning, and even though the request for an early start was one she'd made, she was dreading another fruitless day on the case. She pushed her fingers through her hair, brushing it back from her face, and shifted her gaze to the empty side of the bed. Her arm flung out to her bedside table and she felt for her phone, typing and sending the same message to each member of her team – *How do you like your eggs on a sandwich?* – before she shifted herself upright, and swung her legs round until she was sitting on the edge of her bed. DC Chris Burton was the first to reply – *I like them to run away from me when I start eating* – and Melanie made a note of the request.

She went for a shower and found another response waiting for her by the time she returned, this one from DS Edd Carter: *Eggs? Ew. Bacon. All the bacon.* She added this request to a fresh note on her phone before she grabbed the rest of her gear for the day and left the house.

.   .   .

It was thirty minutes later when Melanie walked into the shared office space of her team, holding a carrier bag that looked full to bursting with sandwiches. DC Lucy Morris was already at her computer screen, frowning over its display, meanwhile Carter was shrugging off his coat. Chris trailed in behind the DI, already mid-conversation with DC Brian Fairer.

'All the bacon?' Melanie said, handing over a small package to Carter. 'Double egg?' she said as she dropped another package onto Chris's desk. The DI walked around the room distributing sandwiches to all the desks until only her own was left in the bag.

'You're like Santa for grown-ups,' Fairer joked, poised to take a bite.

'If she were Santa,' Edd spoke through a mouthful of bread, 'this would be whiskey.'

'She keeps the whiskey in her desk drawer,' Chris said, throwing a wink at her boss who smiled, offering no confirmation or denial – which she knew the team would take note of.

'Right.' Melanie headed to the front of the room. As she turned to a flipchart, positioned alongside the evidence board, DC David Read fell through the office door, audibly panting as though he had run the entire way there.

'Did I miss sandwiches?' he asked the room, and Fairer threw a small wrapped package at his partner by way of providing a response. 'Cracking.' Read took the sandwich over to his desk and took a seat.

'Brilliant,' Melanie said, her voice flat. She turned again to write on the fresh sheet of paper that was pinned in front of her. 'This is what we know,' she said, writing as she spoke. 'The man we currently have in custody is called Steven Knight, thirty-eight, local to the area, although he sometimes works out of the area as a contractor. Early this morning he told one of our PCs that he'd been out of the area for a few days, which is why he hadn't come forward himself.' She faced the team. 'That doesn't quite explain why he went straight to the pub and not to the station, but we'll get to the bottom of that when we question him, which is the plan for this morning. Carter and myself will conduct the preliminary interview to see how the ground lies, meanwhile, Burton,' she said, addressing Chris directly, 'I need you to courier a DNA swab over to the forensics lab as soon as we've taken it from Knight, and they'll push that through as fast as they can.' Melanie paused for confirmation from Chris, who nodded. 'Morris, any more news on that computer?'

'Some,' Lucy said with notable hesitation. 'But there's still stuff coming through.'

Melanie nodded. 'We've got enough for now. Everyone know what they're doing?'

A wave of nods moved around the room before Melanie retreated into her office, taking her untouched sandwich with her.

She had barely finished her breakfast when her desk phone rang. On answering, she found it was the front desk sergeant calling to announce the arrival of Steven Knight's solicitor – earlier than planned, Melanie thought, but she wouldn't make a roadblock of it. She thanked the caller before leaving the office to head down to the interview rooms, grabbing a tired Carter on the way.

'You're sure you're good for this?' Melanie asked.

Edd sighed. 'Jesus, Mel, it's about the only thing I am good for.'

The pair shared a smile before Melanie pushed open the door and both officers stepped inside to find Steven Knight and his solicitor mid-conversation at the interview table. They ceased talking as both officers entered the room and took their seats; Melanie opposite Knight, Edd opposite the man representing him. Melanie set paperwork and a padded envelope on the table between her and the suspect before officially opening the interview. In her experience, people often talked more when they thought you already had evidence against them...

'Mr Knight, I'm DI Watton and this is my colleague DS Carter. You understand that you're here for questioning in relation to the murder of Jenni Grantham?' Melanie asked.

Steven Knight gave a defeated nod before his solicitor stepped in. 'I'd like the record to show that my client is willing to comply with all and any needs that the police might have on this matter.'

'Good to know,' Melanie said, parting the lips of the brown padded envelope that sat on top of her pile. 'We'd like a DNA sample, Mr Knight, if you don't mind. If you do mind–'

'He doesn't mind,' the solicitor cut her off.

Melanie leaned forward and inserted the cotton swab into the open mouth of her suspect. She moved the item along the inside of his cheeks, as instructed, before returning it to the plastic shield that housed it and slipping it back into the envelope.

'What happened between you and Jenni Grantham last week?' Melanie jumped straight into the questioning without missing a beat and Knight was visibly startled. 'We've got footage that shows you were with her, but we can't seem to find evidence of you two actually knowing each other.' Melanie fanned out her papers as she spoke, as though looking for something.

'We didn't know each other,' Knight replied. His voice was flat, cracking around the edges as though he'd spent a long time shouting.

When Melanie looked up, she saw how deflated the man was. He was wearing a custody jumper in a washed-out grey – issued after he'd vomited on himself in the early hours, so Melanie had heard through the grapevine – but the tired look of the jumper matched his overall expression. It might have been sleep deprivation – although Melanie doubted it from the view she'd had of him the previous night – but it could also have been a hangover, tiredness, even a growing concern for his freedom that was weighing the man down. 'We met that evening while I was outside having a smoke.'

'Was she in the pub?' Melanie asked.

Knight shook his head. 'No, she hadn't been in there, not that I'd seen anyway. But she was walking past and that's when I spotted her.' He paused, swallowed hard. 'That's when I grabbed her.' There was a twist in Melanie's stomach at the thought of where this interview might go, but she knew it couldn't be this easy to catch a killer – and Knight's solicitor looked far too relaxed to be representing one. 'I just wanted to talk to her, genuinely. She was a pretty girl, and I was a drunk idiot.'

At least he's honest, Melanie thought. 'You're aware of Jenni's age?'

Knight sighed. 'Now I am, yeah.'

Edd gave his boss a gentle nudge beneath the table. 'She was a pretty girl though, right?' he asked Knight, and the man being questioned shot Edd a suspicious glance. 'We get it.' Edd gave a deliberate look to Melanie and laughed. 'At least, I get it,' he corrected himself.

'If I'd known–'

'But you didn't know, and that's not on you. Plus, it doesn't sound like anything happened, not really, right?' Edd pushed, his tone chatty, light-hearted.

'Right.' Knight agreed cautiously, but there was a notable relief in his voice. 'Literally nothing. I was talking to her, and she freaked out and tried to walk away and because,' he stalled, as if weighing up what he could say next, how he could possibly phrase it. 'Jesus, because I was drunk, and an idiot, I didn't want her to walk away.'

'So, you pulled at her clothing?' Melanie asked, her tone curt, judgemental.

'It wasn't like that, at all. I reached for her, I reached for her arm and she moved as I pulled, and her hoodie just came away. That's literally all that happened.' Knight's tone had changed again, shifting back into something more panicked.

'What happened to her hoodie, Mr Knight?' the DI replied.

'Her hoodie? Christ, she took it. Look, I followed her.' He paused to let out a hard sigh, as if knowing how bad this admission was beginning to sound. 'I took like, three steps forward to give her the hoodie back, she snatched at it, and went. That was all.'

Melanie made a note of Knight's explanation on a blank sheet in front of her before nodding to Edd, giving him the all-clear to continue questioning.

'You had a little chat with her too though, yes?' Edd asked. Melanie flicked through the handful of still shots that had been stripped from the CCTV footage and settled on one that showed Jenni in front of Knight. 'See this one, here,' Edd said, taking the image. 'It looks as though she's shouting something at you, man, like she's really going for it.' Edd moved the image forward so Knight could take a look, and the suspect shot a shielded glance at his solicitor. 'Anything you can tell us about what got said?' Edd pushed.

'No, there isn't,' Knight's solicitor answered. 'Not until we've had time to discuss this between ourselves.' Melanie opened her mouth to object, but the opportunity was robbed from her as the solicitor spoke again. 'My understanding is that you've cautioned my client, but you haven't charged him. If he wants to talk to me in private, he's entitled to do so.'

Melanie collected together the scraps of paper from across the table. 'You're right, you're entitled to talk in private.' She stood, heaving the paperwork up with her. 'Just like we're entitled to hold him for a while longer, and just like we're entitled to interview him again later. Will an hour be long enough for you both?'

The pair exchanged a look. Knight nodded, and his solicitor conceded that an hour would be enough time for them to talk through their next steps. Melanie and Edd excused themselves from the interview room, shutting the door firmly and knocking off the audio feed connected to the room. It killed Melanie to lose her ear on the situation, but rules were rules.

Both officers walked determinedly back up the corridor until they were well out of earshot of any interested PCs.

When they were a comfortable distance away, Edd was the first out of the two of them to crack. 'He's a stupid tosser and I hate him already.'

Melanie exhaled heavily, an almost laugh. 'Can't charge him for that though, can we.'

23

Melanie faced away from the open-plan office space and stared at the evidence board for what felt to Chris Burton like at least five minutes. As requested, Chris had couriered the DNA sample over to forensics where it had been accepted with a glum expression. 'Another rush job, is it?' the technician had asked and Chris had answered in the affirmative, despite the young man's obvious annoyance.

Since arriving back at the station, Melanie had collared Chris to look over any loose ends while Carter excused himself for half an hour of so-called personal business. Both officers were fixated on the board – Melanie more so than Chris – until DC Brian Fairer kicked into life at the back of the room.

'Patrick Nelson,' he said, in an almost-shout.

'What about him?' Melanie asked, turning.

'Did we talk to him?'

Melanie thought for a second and shook her head. 'He was sick, unwell with something earlier in the week. It's only been a couple of days though, and his mother said she'd call.' Melanie turned back to the board to look again at the pictures of Jenni, one in particular jumping out as it featured the friend in question: Patrick Nelson stood one side of their victim, while a beaming Eleanor Gregory stood the other. Melanie thought back to the interview footage from Eleanor's first and only visit; the young girl was more inquisitive than she was sad...

'Did anything strike you as odd about Eleanor Gregory?' Melanie asked, turning to face Chris.

The other officer considered this. 'Not odd, as such. Edd thought it was strange that she wasn't more upset, I think, but it's shock, isn't it? It'll hit her at some point,' Chris replied, shrugging off the question.

But something occurred to Melanie. 'She was quite interested in the station though, how we record the interviews, that sort of thing.'

Melanie rubbed at the back of her neck, fingering the tension that was beginning to stretch up from her shoulder blades. When she looked back at the board, it was as though she couldn't see the evidence at all; instead, one blank space after another jumped out at her, the many holes in Jenni Grantham's storyline. She looked from friends to the search history to Michael Richards' victims, and finally settled on Steven Knight. He knew something, of that much Melanie felt certain, but whether he knew what they needed remained to be seen. Melanie turned back to face the room and called for her colleague's attention.

'Fairer, add a visit to Nelson's house to your list, would you? Try lunchtime and if that doesn't work, go for late afternoon. If Patrick's so ill, he should be there at one time or another.' Her colleague nodded and made a note of something on a sheet in front of him; whatever else got done today, at least Melanie knew that one loose thread would be tied.

It had been an hour and twenty minutes since the first discussion when Melanie stepped back into the interview room, this time accompanied by Chris rather than Edd. Despite numerous phone calls, it looked as though Carter was off the grid and Melanie didn't have time to be put out by it. She'd grabbed her most capable colleague and made fresh introductions on their entry into the room.

'No DS Carter?' Knight's solicitor asked, eyeing Chris up and down.

'He's otherwise engaged, following up on a new lead,' Melanie said with a tight smile; she enjoyed watching Steven Knight flinch at the comment. 'If we may, we've got one or two questions that we'd like to ask.' She paused for their approval. Knight shot a look at his solicitor who nodded and that seemed to be permission enough for the suspect to turn back and face Melanie again. 'Good. For starters, we'd like to know what you and Jenni Grantham were talking about on this film footage.'

Knight let out a slow sigh. 'I don't remember.'

Melanie and Chris shared a sceptical look. 'You don't remember?' Melanie asked, her disbelief creeping through her tone. 'Mr Knight, you remember seeing her, and interacting with her, you even remember disrobing her at one point–'

'Detective Inspector, please, stick to what you're good at. This isn't a courtroom,' the solicitor snapped, and Melanie threw him a look that could land a man six feet under.

Chris flicked through still shots until she found the one of Jenni, arms spread, and mouth contorted into what looked like the beginnings of rage. In the image, Steven Knight could be seen staring at the girl, wearing a near-smirk. Chris laid the image flat on the table and pushed it towards the suspect.

'You're telling us you don't remember what got said here?'

Knight stared down at the image. 'She was angry, I remember that much.'

'I think we could have got there ourselves,' the DI interjected.

'DI Watton, might I remind you that you're yet to charge my client, and by my workings, you've already had him here for a good...' The solicitor paused to check his watch. 'Getting on for eighteen hours, wouldn't you say? Your time might be better spent asking questions, rather than making snide remarks.'

Melanie flashed the same tight smile from earlier. 'Might I remind you, we're entitled to hold a suspect for up to ninety-six hours if the crime they're potentially involved with is of a serious nature.' She paused for a rebuttal, but nothing came. Instead, the solicitor eyed his client and gave Knight a slight nod, as though encouraging something from him. 'Maybe we should start this line of enquiry again, Mr Knight, see if these other images prompt anything for you.' Melanie thumbed through still shots as she spoke, but Knight quickly broke the silence.

'Jesus, she was going somewhere, alright? I don't know where, she didn't tell me. But when I stopped her, she said she couldn't talk because she had somewhere to be, and she was running late. That's as much as I know,' he said, laying his hands flat on the table. 'She was angry because I made her late, and now I wish I'd made her even more bloody late, for all the difference it might have made.' He leaned back in his chair and stared at the table top, avoiding eye contact with the other three individuals in the room, all of whom were looking at him.

'Why didn't you tell us this earlier?' Chris asked.

'Please, I know why I'm here,' he replied, sounding spiteful. 'You think I did it.'

'We don't think anything at this stage, Mr Knight.' Melanie leaned back in her seat to match the man's position. 'But we also can't rule anything out, and you're the last person to see Jenni alive, as it stands. So, naturally...' She let her sentence trail off, lifting her eyes to make contact with the man in front of her. Despite it having only been an hour, Steven Knight looked considerably more tired than he had done earlier in the morning.

'Naturally I'm a suspect?' Knight said.

Chris flipped to a fresh page in her notebook and picked up a pen. 'This would be so easily resolved, you know, if you could just tell us your whereabouts after you saw Jenni. Could you walk us through what happened in the hours after this, perhaps?' Chris pointed to the still shot of them arguing, spread out on the table.

Knight rubbed at his eyes. 'I was in The Black Hound for another hour or so, then I went home. While I was there I would have seen Tony, and Harry, he's the landlord so he'll have been there. Mary might have too, I can't remember.'

Chris allowed him to rattle out one name after another, noting them down as he spoke. When Knight came to an abrupt halt, Chris's head snapped up to take a look at him.

'That's all I've got,' he explained.

'They're people from the pub,' Melanie said. 'What about after that?'

'I already said, I went home.'

'No one can verify that?' the DI pushed, upright in her seat.

'I live alone, who would be able to?'

Melanie threw Chris a look and both officers packed away their respective paperwork. The men opposite them sat in silence throughout the process, and it was only when Melanie pushed her seat back from the table that Knight finally spoke. 'Wait, are we done here?'

'He's free to go?' his solicitor chimed in.

Melanie fought hard to bite back a smile. 'No, I'm afraid not.'

'We'll chase these names up, see how far we get with them. We may need your help if there are people we can't track down,' Chris added.

'But I've got an alibi,' Knight protested.

'Not yet you haven't,' Melanie said, standing as she spoke. 'You're entitled to more time with your solicitor, of course, but I'm afraid we're within our rights to hold you a little while longer while we verify one or two things.'

'What's a little while longer?' Knight's solicitor asked, cutting across his client who had no doubt been about to protest his treatment.

'Until we can verify these alibis and get his DNA dismissed from the suspect pool,' Melanie explained before turning to walk toward the door. 'Knock when you're finished, and the officer outside will see that you both get where you need to be.' The DI opened the door and stepped aside to let her colleague leave the room first, flashing both men a thin smile before exiting. Melanie had been expecting to see a police constable lingering close by but instead, as she pulled the door closed behind her, she nearly stepped into DC Lucy Morris.

'News?' Melanie asked.

'The tech team have finished with Jenni's computer. She was a smart kid, or she was talking to smart people, either way she had things hidden that I couldn't find, and the other team have only found just now. But there are conversations, long and detailed conversations, with someone called...' She paused and checked her hand, the relevant information hastily scribbled across her left palm. 'With someone going by the user name The Real Michael Richards.'

24

JenniGRR:
 So we'll do on it Halloween

TheRealMichaelRichards:
 Makes sense to me
 I think it'll have the most impact that way too

JenniGRR:
 In the evening yeah

TheRealMichaelRichards:
 Yeah
 Doing it in the daytime won't get much attention
 Plus people will find you in the morning
 Think what a shock that will be haha

· · ·

Melanie set the transcript down and stared across the desk to DS Edd Carter, DC Chris Burton, and DC Lucy Morris. The DI had been reading the document aloud for the benefit of the former two officers, but Morris had stared on passively, already familiar with the contents of the conversations after having spent the last day sifting through their fine details. In that time, Melanie had asked Steven Knight for access to his computer and, to her genuine disappointment, he'd complied with the request. His laptops – work and personal – were in the capable hands of the force's tech team and so far they had found two fifths of nothing.

'I can't make any fucking sense of this,' the DI announced.

'Was she planning her own murder with someone?' Chris asked tentatively, knowing how ridiculous the question would sound.

'Who would do that?' Carter chimed in. 'Why would Jenni do that? She was a good kid.'

'We keep saying that, Carter, but we're not seeing a huge amount of evidence towards it.' Melanie stood from her desk and paced about the small space that the furniture afforded her. She pushed her fingertips hard into her forehead and exhaled deeply. 'Okay, we need to think about this logically; what else do we have between Jenni and this online character?'

Lucy shuffled through the pile of papers in front of her and began to read.

JenniGRR:

Why do we need a practice run though
I mean how hard can it be haha

TheRealMichaelRichards:

Better to be safe than found out
Right?

Jen are you still there?

JenniGRR:

Sorry Mum came in

Yeah I guess you're right

Just seems like a lot of effort

When did you want to do it?

Lucy halted her reading of the transcript. 'Between the two of them, they plan for whatever the practice run is to take place four nights after the night Jenni actually died. At least, that's what their conversation suggests. But there's a later conversation.' She paused to thumb through documents. 'Yep, this one, a later one, only by a day or so, where Jenni asks a particularly interesting question.'

JenniGRR:

Why are you using that screen name anyway?

TheRealMichaelRichards:

What do you mean?

JenniGRR:

I mean what I say

You've set up a new account just for this?

TheRealMichaelRichards:

I want it to be authentic

Just in case

Melanie sank down into her chair. 'She was on good terms with whoever is behind this screen name, that's what we're getting from this?' Lucy nodded by way of a response. 'I don't know what we're meant to do with that,' Melanie announced to the room, her head balanced on her balled-up fist. 'We're going to have to take this to her parents, see how much they knew about her online habits, who she was likely to have been talking to on any given evening. Burton, you're with me.' Melanie paused to check her watch. 'It's a sociable enough hour to pay them a visit. Meanwhile, Carter, can you get over to the forensics lab and push them for DNA answers. They respond better face to face.' Edd rolled his eyes and Melanie stopped at the gesture. 'Oh, I'm sorry, do you have somewhere else to be?' Her tone was cutting and Edd looked visibly startled by it.

'No,' he replied. 'No, this is no problem at all.'

Melanie eyed Lucy Morris. 'How long will it take for tech to pull Knight's computer records, past conversations and all that?'

Lucy shrugged. 'He handed over his passwords, so the surface look-through shouldn't take too long. They'll dig deeper, of course, to see if they can find any of this stuff buried.' She gestured with the conversation scripts as she spoke. 'Jenni's conversations were well hidden on her laptop, but it was the person on the other side of the screen who talked her through it, so they'll dredge through everything Knight has got to find something that matches this.'

'Can you be helping them?' Melanie asked.

Another shrug. 'Probably?'

'You're excused from the office for the day. Get over there, see what you can push them for. Knight isn't looking good for this, I know, but we've got another fourteen hours with him and I'm sure as shit not letting him leave this station until we can give the

Granthams a definite answer on what he did and didn't do to their daughter.'

Carter and Morris excused themselves, leaving Burton behind.

'Are you good for this?' Melanie asked, tugging on her jacket.

'Why wouldn't I be?' Chris flashed a smile. Melanie could always tell when her colleague was struggling with a case and this time was no exception. Of course it bothered Chris that their victim was a young woman – a child, really – but Melanie knew she couldn't let that side of her feelings show if she stood a chance of being taken more seriously. Chris sighed when Melanie smiled in return, grabbed her thinned out copy of the conversation transcripts and headed for the open door of her office, with her junior trailing not too far behind.

By the time Edd pulled up outside of the forensics offices – a gold mine of scientific knowledge that had been tacked onto the local university some three years back – the place was already aflutter with life. There were white coats and students galore around the space, and Edd felt grateful that he knew exactly which office he was making a beeline for. He skimmed through titles as he walked along each corridor, checking the names pinned to the doors as he went along, until he finally ended up outside of the broadly titled "Lab1" where he knocked lightly, and waited to be called in.

'Come on!' came a voice from inside.

When Edd stepped over the threshold he was greeted by the sight of a man, facing away from him, his back arched over as he looked into a small pool of something that was positioned underneath an expensive-looking piece of equipment. Edd felt nervous to take a deep-out breath in case he expanded enough to knock something pricey out of place. He remained fixed to the spot until the man eventually came up for air and turned to face him. To Edd's annoyance, it looked as though he was dealing with a twelve-year-old – a feeling that he experienced more and more frequently these days...

'DC Chris Burton?' the man asked, extending a hand.

Edd reciprocated the gesture. 'Afraid not, DS Edd Carter.'

'We're moving higher up the food chain,' the man replied with a half-laugh. 'ID?'

Edd pulled his badge from his inside pocket and flashed it to his questioner, quietly delighted that the young man had thought to take such a precaution.

'I assume you're after these,' the technician continued their conversation, reaching for a sealed envelope that sat atop a pile of cardboard folders. 'Results from the sample your colleague dropped off, sealed and secured as requested. Do you think you'll be sending any more emergencies our way?' he asked jovially, but Edd detected a hint of sincerity too.

'I hope not, mate,' the officer replied. He took the envelope and began to lift the sealed lip before halting; should this be the DI's job? Unsure, he opted for a different tactic. 'Any chance you know what's in these?'

The technician narrowed his eyes and sucked in his bottom lip, as though debating whether he was at liberty to say. He took a quick look around himself, to ensure that the surrounding lab space was still empty, before giving Edd a shrug.

'What the hell. He's not your man.'

Edd felt the air rush out of him. 'There's no match?'

'Not to the full sample or the partial. Nothing that we pulled from the girl can be physically traced back to your blokey.' The technician gave Edd a half-smile, his mouth pulled down in a despondent expression. 'Better luck next time?' he said, before turning back to his workstation.

25

Melanie and Chris were nearly outside the Granthams' house when Carter called the DI's work phone. It wasn't connected to the car's Bluetooth system so Chris answered on her boss's behalf, a curt, 'Hang on' while she struggled to find the right onscreen logo to activate the speakerphone. Once Edd's breathing was magnified in greater detail, she instructed her colleague to continue.

'It's not a match, boss,' he announced.

'Not to either?'

'Nope, they tested him against the partial and against the complete sample. There's no trace of Knight anywhere on Jenni according to the forensics that are available.'

'Bollocks,' Melanie snapped as the car came to halt at their destination. 'Chase up Morris, would you, Edd? See if she's getting anywhere with the tech team. We'll be letting Knight go before the day is out otherwise.'

Chris extinguished the phone call and, following her boss's lead, stepped out of the car in silence. Melanie was disgruntled by this latest news; another blow to the case that the DI and her team could have done without.

'Are you showing them the transcripts?' Chris asked, breaking the silence as both officers stood outside the front door waiting for admittance.

Melanie sighed. 'I haven't decided yet.'

DC Ian Dixon opened the door and quietly welcomed both officers into the hallway. There was a solemn tone in the house and despite the grief that filled the space, Melanie couldn't help but feel there was something else afoot here. She waited for Dixon to shut the door and pull the lock across before she questioned her young colleague.

'Has something gone on?'

Dixon rubbed at the back of his neck, avoiding eye contact with his superior. 'Bloody press got hold of their temporary phone number, didn't they? Probably some scum or another selling numbers to the highest bidder.' He was obviously annoyed, an angry redness lingered at the edges of his cheeks. 'It's shaken them both up a little, the questions they were asking about Jenni, the allegations.' Dixon shook his head, signalling the end of the conversation before gesturing down the hallway, allowing Melanie to take the lead. The living room door was pulled firmly closed so she pressed forward to the kitchen. Inside that room, she found both Robert and Evie Grantham sitting opposite each other, cradling their respective cups of tea with what seemed like little interest in actually drinking the beverages. Melanie wondered how many cups of tea Dixon must have made in the ten days.

'Mr and Mrs Grantham, I hope you don't mind us dropping in like this,' Melanie said. Without a word, Robert stood from his chair and gestured for Melanie to take the seat; he shuffled across, taking the chair next to his wife, leaving another seat in the middle free for Chris.

With all four individuals settled around the table – Dixon hovering in the doorway like an angelic figure – Melanie continued. 'I've brought my colleague DC Burton with me today, as she's also working closely with me on Jenni's case, and we were wondering whether we might be able to discuss one or two new developments with you.'

'Please,' Evie said, her voice a faded version of the one Melanie remembered.

'We've been looking through Jenni's computer records, as you know, and I was wondering whether you might know who she was talking to on the Internet, or friends she often mentioned talking to perhaps? There are a couple of conversations under screen names and we're having a hard time pinning down who's who,' Melanie said, trying to sound less eager than she felt for their answers.

Robert flashed down-turned lips and looked to his wife.

'There were so many,' she said, dropping her head into her hands. For the seconds that followed, the woman remained quiet until, with a sudden burst of energy, her head snapped up. 'Have you spoken to her friends about this; Eleanor, and that Patrick boy? The three of them always seemed to be chatting in one place or another.'

'Did they talk online, do you know?' Chris pushed, her notebook in hand to write down anything of interest or use.

'I imagine so, like I said, they seemed to be talking everywhere, all the bloody time.'

Melanie could sense the shift in Evie's grief; shock turning to anger at what had happened to her child, at what was continuing to happen to her. Melanie felt a strong sympathy for the grieved mother – but they still needed their answers.

'So, it was only people that you're familiar with, people she mentioned in real life? There weren't any new names, or names that she only mentioned in relation to talking to online, nothing like that that you can recall?' Melanie asked, her tone firm. She felt like she was reframing the same question in different ways, but they had to be sure that they weren't missing something – something that could unlock the case entirely.

'Like chat rooms, is that what you're asking?' Robert asked.

Chris made a quick note – *chat rooms?* – on her pad. It was something that they hadn't talked about in any serious detail, but it was certainly worth considering – especially if the parents weren't able to shed any light on who their daughter was talking to.

'Not necessarily. We're just wondering whether Jenni had any friends that she exclusively knew and spoke to via the Internet, rather than having any face-to-face interaction with them.' Melanie's patience was beginning to fray, but she had to remind herself why they were here, what they were doing – what their interviewees had recently been through. Melanie sighed lightly. 'Did she use chat rooms, do you know?' The tech team hadn't found evidence for this, but it was still worth asking, if only to keep the Granthams in the right frame of mind for questions.

'When she was younger,' Evie admitted. 'I think she found them by accident, to be honest, and we stopped her as soon as we found out what she was doing, gave her the lecture about online dangers and that sort of thing. But she was a young woman, her phone attached to her hand, you know how it is.'

'Truthfully, detectives, we didn't monitor our daughter's online behaviour,' Robert said, cutting across his own speech with a bitter laugh. 'Although it seems that perhaps it would have been a good idea to.' The couple shared a look before Robert reached over to wrap an arm around his wife's shoulders. They were closer than they had been on previous visits, Melanie noted, and something about the observation pleased her.

'I appreciate this is a difficult time for you,' Melanie said. 'But if you do think of anything, anyone Jenni might have mentioned, even if it was just in passing, it would be a great help to us.' The Granthams just about held eye contact with the officer but neither of them could bring themselves to say anything. Melanie gave a sad smile before pushing her chair back from the table. 'Thank you both for your time again today. I hope we'll have something a little more concrete for you soon.'

Dixon moved to one side to allow his colleagues to step through the doorway, but Evie Grantham called them back into the room. 'The man, the one you've got in custody.' The two officers turned back into the kitchen to face the woman. Melanie appeared impassive, neutral, but there was an anxious twist in her lower stomach. 'He isn't the one who did it, is he?' Despite the cracks around the edges of her voice, Evie Grantham sounded strong, determined, and neither officers could bring themselves to skirt around the truth.

'It doesn't look like it, no,' Melanie admitted. Robert dropped his head toward the table, but Evie held eye contact with the DI. 'I'm sorry, we are–'

'We know,' Evie cut across her. 'We know you're trying.'

Dixon saw both officers to the front door then, allowing the Granthams a moment to themselves. The three said their goodbyes and Melanie and Chris quietly paced back to their car, parked at the end of the driveway. Neither moved for a moment, wrapped up in their respective thoughts about the couple, the case, the young woman at the centre of it all.

'We need those kids back in,' Melanie announced.

'Eleanor Gregory?'

'And Patrick Nelson. I don't care which end things are coming out of, he's coming in,' Melanie said, her tone curt, defiant as she inserted the key fob into the car and fired up the engine. She checked the time on the dashboard clock before she pulled away from the curb. 'Call Fairer, tell him to get over to the Nelsons' house and pull Patrick in. I don't want any excuses this time. You can give Carter a call too, and he can grab Eleanor and a parent as college wraps up. I want them both questioned as soon as possible.' Melanie pressed down hard on the accelerator, speeding toward the junction at the end of the road where she braked hard enough to lift Chris forward in her seat. Melanie looked left, right, left again before pulling out of the road, talking as the car turned. 'Someone must know something about Jenni sodding Grantham.'

26

DS Edd Carter had been parked outside of Eleanor Gregory's house for nearly thirty minutes. He'd seen her mother appear in front of one window or another a handful of times while he'd been waiting, but he didn't want to strike until he knew both individuals were home. He checked his watch again; Eleanor finished college forty minutes earlier, and there was still no sign of her. He hoped that she wasn't the sort of girl to engage in after-school clubs and social circles; although, from the young woman's initial interview, she seemed more focused on her friendship with Patrick and Jenni than with anyone else.

Again, Edd let out a hard sigh as Mrs Gregory crossed in front of the living room window, this time with a phone pressed to her ear. She took a pointed look out of the front window but seemed to look right through Edd, and the officer, relieved not to have been spotted, hoped that it was her daughter on the other end of the phone – hoped even more that her mother was ordering her home within the next ten minutes, or else Edd's working day could turn into a complete washout.

Edd imagined DC Fairer, somewhere across town, going through the same long-winded waiting game, although at least his pick up should have been at home, given that all reports pointed to Patrick being too ill to leave the house. Edd pulled his mobile phone from his inside pocket and thumbed down to his colleague's name. If they were both waiting it out, they may as well make the most of this time for a catch up, Edd thought. The dial tone sounded out ring after ring until eventually cutting through to Fairer's voicemail. Edd decided against leaving a message when he spotted a young woman, sporting what was distinctly a college hoodie – they had studied the design so many damn times – round the corner into the cul-de-sac. At this distance he couldn't immediately tell whether it was Eleanor Gregory or not, but he wanted to be ready to approach if it turned out to be her.

As the young woman lessened the gap between herself and the observing officer, Edd determined that yes, it was Eleanor Gregory, finally heading for home. The teenager appeared to be in her own little world – head down, staring at something on her mobile phone screen – so she passed Edd's car without so much as an upward glance. Masterfully, she unlocked the front door without looking up from whatever held her attention, and she stepped over the threshold into the family home without even double-checking her footing. Edd shook his head at the observation. When had he got to an age where these things stood out to him? Unwilling to linger on that thought for too long, he replaced his phone in his inside pocket and exited the vehicle, making a quick step in the direction of the Gregorys' house.

If Mrs Gregory had spotted Edd – which she must have done, he thought – then she hadn't given any signs of it during her looks through different windows. However, Edd was a good five paces away from the front door when it swung open, the unimpressed-looking lady of the house standing in the doorway, just waiting for a visitor it seemed. Edd flashed a half-smile, half-laugh as he came to a stop on the doormat.

'You aren't undercover, are you?' Mrs Gregory asked, her delivery flat.

Edd couldn't help but crack a smile. 'No, apparently I'm not stealthy enough.'

'You'd better come in.' Without waiting for a reply, the woman turned away from the open door and backstepped up her hallway. Thrown by the invitation – or was it a demand, really? – Edd stepped into the house, closed the door behind him, and followed the path just trodden by the homeowner. At the end of the corridor and through an open door, Edd found Mrs Gregory leaning against a kitchen work surface with her daughter, Eleanor, sitting at the kitchen table at the centre of the room.

'May I?' Edd asked, gesturing toward an empty chair at the table and Mrs Gregory gave a curt nod of approval. He positioned himself opposite Eleanor who, so much for her excited demeanour the first time around, looked tired, troubled even. The young woman refused to make eye contact with Edd and he wondered what had changed from the first talk to this one. 'Everything okay, Eleanor?' he asked, his tone gentle.

The young woman looked up. 'Has something else happened?' Her voice cracked halfway through the sentence and, as though sensing her daughter's need, Mrs Gregory appeared with a glass of water for her child. Eleanor sipped at the drink before speaking again. 'I mean, have you found something else?'

'Sort of. We've found some things on Jenni's computer–'

'The search terms?' Eleanor cut across him, showing the enthusiasm that he recognised from their previous encounter, albeit a fraction of what it was.

'Something else. There are conversations between Jenni and someone.'

'Who?' Eleanor snapped without missing a beat.

'That's what we're hoping you can tell us. Do you know of anyone she was talking to online, maybe? Or even someone at college who she spoke to a lot via the net, anything like that?' Edd asked, cautious not to put words in the girl's mouth but conscious that teenagers sometimes needed the grown-ups to do the thinking for them.

Eleanor seemed to really consider this before answering. 'I can't remember her mentioning anyone, no.'

'Is that all then?' Mrs Gregory chimed in, no sooner had her daughter answered.

'Not quite,' Edd said, addressing the mother before turning back to the daughter. 'How would you feel about coming down to the station again? We've got some things we'd like for you to take a look at, and we can have a chat in the interview room.' Edd was mindful of his tone slipping into toddler territory, taking on the same level of patronising that he typically only reserved for Emily when she was being especially difficult. He straightened himself up a touch before continuing. 'Your mother would be there as well, of course.'

'Does she have to do this?' Mrs Gregory asked.

'We're not charging her with anything, if that's what you mean,' Edd replied, knowing that it wasn't at all what the girl's mother had meant, but also knowing what the impact of mentioning charges would be. When he looked back to Eleanor, she was still downcast, and Edd couldn't help but wonder what had prompted such a change in just a few days.

'Honestly, DS Carter, I think Eleanor has been through enough recently.'

'I understand that, I do,' Edd said, standing to address Mrs Gregory directly. 'But if we stand a chance of catching Jenni Grantham's killer, we're going to need Eleanor's help. I'm sorry to put her and you in this position.' He wasn't sorry at all, and as for putting Eleanor in this position, she seemed to have previously enjoyed the excitement of being in a police station, so Edd had to hope that when she returned to the interview room, the same engagement that they were gifted with the last time would reappear.

Both mother and daughter swapped a guarded look. Eventually Mrs Gregory asked her daughter: 'What do you think, El, are you up to it?'

In a bid to offer additional support – or rather, encouragement – Edd chimed in again. 'We'll be bringing Patrick in as well, so it's not like you'll be going through this on your own.'

The colour from Eleanor's face drained, as though someone had uncorked her. She looked hard at Edd for a second, her eyes narrowing while a redness crept up from beneath the collar of her jumper, slowly spreading across her neck and up to the back edges of her cheeks. She gave her head a firm shake before turning to look at her mother, and when Edd followed the young woman's stare, he found her mother's expression was also one of confusion. Eleanor looked from her parent back to the officer in front of her and stammered, 'P-Patrick? You mean, you've found him?'

DC Brian Fairer stood at the front door of the Nelson house, straightening out his tie while he waited for someone to respond to his second knock. Before his knuckles could make contact with the door for a third time, someone pulled it open with a curtness that startled the officer. In the doorway there stood a middle-aged man with bags for life beneath his eyes and a thin layer of grease forming over the front of his hair, and it crossed Fairer's mind that he might have the wrong house altogether.

'Mr Nelson?' the officer offered, half-expecting denial from the man.

'Are you with the police?' Despite the man's physical abruptness, his tone was much softer, with a hint of desperation that Fairer hadn't been anticipating. 'Do you have something? Is there news?'

Fairer was taken aback. 'I'm sorry, I don't–' he started but Mr Nelson cut across him.

'You'd better come in.'

The man disappeared into the house and from the open door, Fairer watched as he walked through the second doorway on the left side of the hall.

When seconds had passed, it seemed unlikely that the man would make a miraculous return so Fairer followed him in, closing the door behind him and following the steps into what turned out to be the living room. On the sofa, the man sat with his arm around a woman – one who Fairer thankfully recognised as Mrs Nelson, from his previous attempt at coaxing Patrick out of the house. The woman was clearly distraught, her face pock-marked with small patches of red, meanwhile tears continued to run down her face quicker than she could catch them. She looked up to Fairer with the same unexpected desperation that he'd noted from her husband. Mrs Nelson opened her mouth as though to speak but a dry croak emerged, followed by a fresh bout of tears.

Fairer rubbed at the back of his neck, scanning the room for clues of what the hell was happening here. He crossed the room to the other sofa and lowered himself down onto it, to sit face to face with the troubled couple. Despite his desire not to look like a total amateur, Fairer had to come clean.

'Mr and Mrs Nelson, I'm afraid I've walked into something that I'm not sure about here.' He paused, adjusted his tie, and took a deep breath before continuing. 'In the Major Incident Team, we're not always kept up to speed on day-to-day cases and I've got to hold my hands up and say that it looks like there are some crossed wires, or missed steps, or – well, something,' he said, running out of filler phrases. 'The reason that I'm here is actually to talk to Patrick, if he's feeling better. We could really use him at the station this evening.'

Mrs Nelson looked at Fairer with a wide-eyed expression before succumbing to another wave of tears. She pressed her face against her husband's chest and pulled his arm tighter around her, as though she were seeking physical protection from Fairer's questions. Meanwhile, Mr Nelson showed no such need for protection; his cheeks were bloated with air and his face reddening, and had he not been holding his wife then Fairer would have been preparing himself for a fist-fight of some description by now.

Holding in his frustration, to some degree, Mr Nelson managed to force out: 'Are you taking the piss?' His tone rid of the earlier desperation, replaced by annoyance, and hurt. 'Jesus Christ, are you all sitting about with your thumbs up your arses? Too busy to find a missing lad, too busy to solve a murder?'

Fairer pulled back, as though recoiling from the words. 'A missing lad?'

Mrs Nelson cracked, lifting her head from her resting pose and said – or rather, shrieked: 'Patrick. Our lad. Our Patrick. Missing!'

Fairer shot Mr Nelson a panicked look before letting his eyes drop down to the man's wife, who had collapsed back into her earlier position. The whole situation dawned on Fairer in a vicious wave: the early desperation, the hope of news, the tears, the bags, the tension...

Patrick Nelson was missing.

27

Melanie slammed her empty mug down on the desk as though she were dropping a gavel. 'This is utter bollocks.' Superintendent Archer looked taken aback by the DI's outburst, but she did nothing to stop the flow of her junior officer once it had started. 'You knew we were running a murder investigation up there, you knew that kids from the college were involved, one of the victims, in fact, and you keep something like this to yourselves?' Melanie unleashed her frustration on DS Ken Fern from the Missing Persons department, who simply sat there and took the criticisms as though he had been expecting them from the off, which made Melanie all the more irritated. 'My men looked like total arses out there yesterday–'

'That's not unusual though,' Ken cut across her, speaking for the first time and leaving Melanie wide-eyed and tight-lipped as she tried to hold in a cutting comeback.

Superintendent Archer leaned forward in her seat, as though preparing to physically put herself between the two officers. 'I think that's quite enough,' she said, before another insult could be launched. 'Fern, you know you were out of order on this,' she said, leaving a beat of silence as though she expected a response despite not having asked a question. When Fern didn't offer an answer, Archer pushed, 'Or do you think your actions were justified?'

The DS paused, as if weighing up his options before answering. 'With all due respect, Ma'am, you're giving us a bit too much credit for how malicious we've been here. It's a young lad who's done a bunk from his parents and as for the murder link, a lot of kids go to that college. I don't think it's as much of a personal attack from my team as Watton, DI Watton, seems to be taking it.'

'He's best friends with the murder victim,' Melanie added, her voice taut.

'Obviously if we'd known that–'

'Which you would have done, had you made us aware of the report that he was missing.'

'We'll go in circles on this all day, officers,' Archer refereed again. 'Fern, whether it was intentional or not, you'll hand over everything that you've got to DI Watton and her team, assuming that you do have something.' Melanie smiled at the cutting remark, but DS Fern seemed not to have even noticed it. 'Whatever case file you've put together, I want the Major Incident Team to have it before the morning is out.' She looked up to her clock. 'That gives you an hour, and if you can't do that, you'll be back in here by the afternoon.'

'The whole case?' Fern asked, clearly taken aback by the request.

'Problem?' Archer replied, her attention already breaking away to the paperwork that covered her desk in a patchwork pattern.

'A little problem, Ma'am, yes, it's a Missing Persons' case.'

'Not anymore it's not,' she said, lifting a single sheet of paper for closer inspection. 'Now it's MIT, and you'll respect that decision, and you'll have the folders ready within the hour. Or...' She trailed out and glanced to Fern for him to provide the missing words.

'Or I'll be back in here by the afternoon.'

'Bingo.' She set the sheet of paper down and picked up another. 'You're excused.'

Melanie and DS Fern stood from their seats but Archer eyed

Melanie with a raised eyebrow. 'You're staying, there are things to discuss.' Melanie deliberately didn't look at Fern; she knew the expression he'd be wearing would be one of smug judgement, and she had no patience for it.

When he'd seen himself out of the room, closing the door with a firm bang, Archer gave Melanie her full attention. 'Where are we with Knight?'

Melanie sighed. 'We're going to have to release him, Ma'am.'

'Because?'

'DNA match, or lack thereof, and there's no evidence to place him as the person Jenni was talking to online either.'

The superintendent lowered her head and, with each hand, rubbed hard at the patches of skin either side of her eyes. When she looked back up to Melanie, the DI saw for the first time just how tired her superior was.

'No chance of that changing?' Archer pushed.

'DC Morris is still in possession of Knight's laptops, but she's gone through them thoroughly with the tech team and there's nothing. I'm assured there are one or two things left to check but, given the type of PC user that Knight is, Morris is quite sure that he doesn't know the ins and outs of a system enough to hide things the way Jenni did.' Melanie had finished but her boss seemed to be waiting for more. 'That being said, we did learn that Jenni was in a rush to meet someone and to get somewhere, which tells us more about her state of mind than we knew before speaking to Knight.'

Archer didn't look convinced, but she pressed on all the same. 'Now another college student seems to have been targeted though. So, what are we thinking here?'

In the absence of a concrete answer, Melanie opted for honesty. 'I don't know, Ma'am. Knight isn't good for it, we're all certain of that much. It's a concern that Patrick Nelson has become involved in this way because honestly, I thought he and the Eleanor girl knew more than they were letting on, but now...' She petered out, trying to order her thoughts before finishing. 'It's a growing concern that someone is going to, or has started to, target college kids. It complicates the Michael Richards involvement, of course, because he never abducted his victims, so it may be that the Michael Richards link was a coincidence to begin with, or it may be that Patrick's disappearance is entirely unrelated, or–'

'You're having too many maybes and ors, Detective Inspector.'

'It's been nearly two weeks, Ma'am,' Melanie said, by way of defending herself. 'We'll get there, we just need the right break.' Although Melanie couldn't deny that she was worried. Whoever had killed Jenni Grantham had been clever and calculated and, whether they'd left clues or not, they were far too intricate to be understood at just one glance. But Melanie knew herself and she knew her team, and she had to believe that they would find – something. 'Rest assured, we're giving everything we've got to this. Now we've got the Nelson case as well, we can look at that alongside Jenni's case and build up.'

Archer looked at her with narrowed eyes, as though inspecting Melanie for something. The DI expected another grilling, or at the very least a cutting remark, but in the end her superior quietly dismissed her with a good luck. 'And you know where I am.'

Edd Carter dragged the spare table from the back corner of the room and placed it alongside the one Chris Burton had already cleared for use. As soon as the tables were pieced together, Melanie up-ended the box of evidence that had been delivered by PC Emerett on behalf of Missing Persons just five minutes earlier.

'Is there anything else I can do for you, DI Watton?' the young PC had asked.

Melanie, her face already buried in the box before her, replied, 'You can tell DS Fern that he's a coward.' After that, she dismissed the officer and called her team to attention to dig through the early findings of their colleagues.

However, when the contents of the box were spread out across two tables, Melanie saw that one table – or maybe even half a desk – would have been just fine. Different members of Melanie's team – Carter, Burton, Fairer, and Read – grabbed at a sheet or bundle of paper apiece, leaving nothing left for the DI herself. While she waited for their early summaries, Melanie turned her attention over to the evidence board. Alongside a smiling Jenni Grantham, there was pictured a beaming Patrick Nelson, his blond hair spiked with too much gel and his mouth pulled into a wide grin. If anyone were to look, they'd find three happy kids in that photograph; but with one dead and one missing, Melanie had to admit that she felt a flutter of panic at what fate might be waiting for Eleanor if they didn't move quickly enough.

'It's been two days,' Carter said. 'Two days since he went missing, and there's allegedly a FLO at the house already.'

'Which there wasn't,' Fairer added.

'Nelson told his mother that he was going out, without notice or prior warning to her–'

'Is that weird, for a teenager?' Read interrupted Edd.

'I mean, if she's commented on it, it must be weird for Patrick. He went out and told her that he couldn't stop to talk because he had somewhere important to be, and he was late.' Edd lifted his head from the sheet and locked eyes with the DI. 'Sound familiar?'

'It's also what Jenni told Knight,' Melanie filled in.

'I've got the father's statement here,' Burton chimed, her face still angled toward the sheet. 'I'd heard Patrick on the phone to someone about five minutes before he left,' Burton read verbatim from the evidence. 'I couldn't hear what was being said but he sounded off, like his voice was rising a bit, I suppose. After that I heard him leave his bedroom and walk downstairs, which I didn't think anything of, and a minute or so later the front door shut. When I went downstairs again my wife told me that Pat had gone out and that he didn't seem right, but honestly, we didn't think much more of it. We put it down to a fight with a friend...' Chris petered out. 'It goes on from there but there's nothing revolutionary really.'

There was a lump of something in Melanie's chest as she saw all eyes turn to her, her team waiting for guidance. An hour and a half earlier, she had total faith in their abilities; she needed some more of that faith.

'Right,' she said, leaning on the table to address them. 'Carter, you're with me, we're going to interview Patrick's parents and we're going to do it properly. I'll drive. On the way you can check the status of a FLO. Burton?' she said, pulling her DC's attention. 'I want you to contact DC Morris, get her back here and tell her we need another round of CCTV coverage. If both of you are on it, God willing we'll find something faster the second time around. Read and Fairer, I want you to get over to the college. Call ahead if you want, or don't, either way Gibbons should co-operate with us at this point; one student dead and another missing can't be doing anything for his reputation. Are we all clear on where we're at?'

She made eye contact with each member of the team, checking one by one that they understood their instructions and one by one the officers left their posts and moved to make a start on their jobs. But Melanie couldn't let them go without one final motivator. 'Detectives,' she said, waiting for their attention to settle on her. 'I don't want another body on that board.'

28

DC Lucy Morris was well into her second hour of watching CCTV footage when she first spotted Patrick Nelson. His coat collar was pulled up high around his neck to protect him from the cutting wind, and he was staring down at his phone as he was walking. When the order had come through to check CCTV footage again, Morris had quickly called around all the shops who had obliged her request without hassle the first time around. She didn't quite have enough volunteers to piece together Nelson's movements after this, but at least she'd found him somewhere. Morris paused the image and pushed herself away from her desk, standing and crossing to Chris Burton who was watching footage from outside The Black Hound, taken over the last two nights. Burton looked bored to within an inch of her life, so Morris settled down next to her to break the news. When her colleague's face was level with her own, Morris announced, 'Got him.'

They both retreated to Morris's desk at a quick pace to watch the footage that she'd found. Their eyes fixed on the screen with great concentration, they watched as Patrick Nelson appeared from the top of the shot, walking along the pavement that ran parallel to a string of shops just outside of the main city centre. They marvelled at the clear view of his face, the worried expression, the boyish nerves that were noticeable just from the way he carried himself, and as he disappeared from shot in the bottom of the frame, Chris let out a deep sigh.

'Pull up Street View, would you?' Chris asked her colleague and Morris followed orders. 'And go to the search box.'

'Woolham Street?' Morris suggested, reciting the street name that this most recent footage had come from. Chris nodded along while Morris input their destination. 'I like the way you think,' the one officer complimented the other as they waited for the street to line up in front of them. 'Got a pen?' Morris asked, zooming in on the shop that the footage had come from. 'So, this is Lavish, which is where we've picked up Patrick. I'm not too worried about the shops in between because we can already see that he's on his own, but if we click this way...' She guided the cursor back along the street. 'We'll find the end shop.'

'Which presumably means finding the direction that he came from?'

'Precisely,' Morris replied, still waiting for the image to shift further along the street. 'So that end of the street starts with Noodle Hut. Can you note that down?' When Morris turned to her colleague, she spotted that Chris was already midway through writing the name, and she couldn't help but smile at her colleague's enthusiasm. Turning back to the screen, she clicked her way in the opposite direction along the same street. 'Whatever the shop is this end will hopefully be able to show us which way Patrick branched off. It could narrow down where he was heading, maybe.' Morris wasn't fully optimistic about the plan, but it was the best idea they had.

'Harris Studios,' Chris read as the pixelated image cleared to reveal the brilliant white outside of what appeared to be a photography studio. She noted down their name. 'You'd think somewhere like that would pride themselves on having photographic evidence of things, right?' Chris tore the sheet of paper out of her notebook and ripped it down the middle, handing Morris the piece that read *Noodle Hut*. 'You take the one end, I'll take the other.'

DCs Read and Fairer took their seats opposite Mr Gibbons; the latter of the gentlemen was in the middle of a phone call and he gestured to the officers with one outstretched finger, promising that just another minute would do the trick. Read took a hard look around the office space – it was a long time since he'd been somewhere like this – and when he dropped his eyes back down, Fairer shot him a questioning look.

'Spotted something?' he mouthed and Read shook his head.

'Right, detectives,' Gibbons said, slamming the phone down with a bang. 'Now that shit show is over for the time being, we can get cracking on this one.' Both officers were clearly taken aback, prompting Gibbons to let out a heavy sigh and add, 'Apologies, two attacks on students in the space of two weeks has left the parents running scared and I'm fencing phone calls about whether their children are even safe to come in.' He paused and rubbed hard at his eyes before continuing. 'It's not as though they've been taken on my watch, is it?'

'We did wonder whether this would be causing you problems,' Read said gently.

'That's an understatement.'

'Is attendance down, would you say?' Fairer asked, pen poised to take notes.

'A little, I suppose,' Gibbons admitted. 'What can I do for you exactly, officers? I'm conscious of wasting yours and my time.'

Despite phrasing it as though he were doing everyone a favour, Gibbons looked less kind and more eager to get this process over with – but why, was the big question.

'We wanted to know how the students were, really,' Read replied, sounding inappropriately relaxed. 'Whether there was any acting out, not turning up, generally not being themselves, anything like that.' On the way over here, Read and Fairer had discussed tactics and decided to be as least threatening as possible, and Read was making a fine job of it. Their brief was to spot any odd behaviours; good students who had suddenly slipped in attendance, or concentration. In short, they were looking for their guilty party.

In response to Read's tone, Gibbons seemed to relax slightly too. 'I actually wish that there was,' he said, his voice suddenly tired. 'That's the thing, nothing and no one has changed. There haven't been any red flags on the school computers, no one messing about on sites they shouldn't be on, that sort of thing, because we do keep an eye on that, you know?' he said, as though looking for credit. Fairer tried on an impressed face that prompted the principal to continue. 'But no, no one is acting out. In fact, the handful of students we have who typically act out have been even quieter than usual. I suppose something about this whole business has just knocked the wind out of them.'

'And who would you say the culprits are for acting out?' asked Read.

Gibbons shook his head. 'Officer, when I say acting out, I mean they aren't concentrating in class or they won't put their bloody phones away. It's a far cry from murder and kidnap. Besides, didn't your DI cover all of this business with the students?'

'Still,' Fairer intervened. 'We're giving things a second look. It's always wise to check.'

'Top of the list is Eleanor Gregory, but she's settled down without her cronies,' Gibbons said, sounding genuinely saddened by the admission. 'Chloe Wentworth, Jacob Bells, Laurie Campbell. Oh, Alistair House, as I said to your DI, was obviously sweet on Jenni Grantham. He hasn't had much to say for himself since this all happened though.' Gibbons continued to rattle off a dozen more names while Fairer struggled to keep up with the spellings. They might be nothing, but they were worth a shot, the DC decided. 'But like I said, officers, none of them are murderers, and even they aren't their usual loud mouth selves while all of this is happening. Christ, Eleanor can just about come in.'

'Is she in today, do you know?' Read asked.

'I'm afraid not, no. She tried to come in, is my understanding, but her mother said she was too panicked to get the whole way here when it came to it. Poor girl, she's lost the most of all of the students in this.'

Fairer took over. 'Patrick Nelson, was he one of the louder students, would you say?'

Gibbons gave the question some real thought before answering. 'Yes,' he eventually admitted. 'But only when he was in the right company.'

Mrs Nelson had collapsed in a mound of tears in the front porch of her house after answering the door and finding Melanie Watton and Edd Carter outside. The struggling mother was convinced that her boy was dead, and that this was the announcement she'd been waiting for. But Melanie talked her round – 'No, Mrs Nelson, not at all, not at all.' – and eventually guided her into the living room, where Mr Nelson was sitting. Scrunched up toward one end of the sofa as though trying to occupy as little space as possible, the man sat with his hands pressed between his knees and his eyes, glazed over, as though he were blissfully unaware of the commotion that had happened just for the officers to get this far into the house. Mr Nelson's attention didn't snap back until his wife laid a gentle hand on his shoulder and gave a slight squeeze, pulling him into the conversation.

'There are new detectives here,' she announced, her voice still shaken from the tears.

'DI Melanie Watton, and this is my colleague DS Edd Carter,'

Melanie said, as her and Edd took a seat on the chairs positioned opposite the large sofa. Out of nowhere, Melanie suddenly felt quite tired of sitting in darkened living rooms, talking to troubled parents, asking about their children...

Edd continued. 'We'd like to go over some of the things that the first detectives will have mentioned. Would that be okay?' Both parents nodded but didn't go as far to offer verbal approval. 'Okay, we have it down here that Patrick went out, telling you that he had somewhere to be. How did he seem when he told you that? Calm, agitated?'

Mrs Nelson thought for a second. 'He sounded worried, that's what I'd say. His voice,' she paused and swallowed in a hard gulp. 'His voice was a little shaken, and I was going to ask – going to ask what the matter was, but he was gone before I even had the chance.'

'So, he was rushing to get somewhere.' Edd spoke while writing.

'To see someone,' Mrs Nelson added and Melanie locked eyes with her.

'No mention of who?' Melanie pushed, hoping for more than Missing Persons had managed in their time here.

'No, he did say,' Mrs Nelson spoke, her tone confused. 'I told the other officers.'

'I'm sorry?' Edd said, looking up from his notes. He shared a worried look with Melanie. 'You know who Patrick was meeting?'

'Michael,' Mr Nelson chimed in, his voice cracking from under-use. 'My wife, she told the officers that Patrick was going to meet someone–'

'I told them Patrick was meeting someone called Michael,' Mrs Nelson cut across her husband. 'But we don't know who Michael is.'

No, Melanie thought with a hard sigh, *and neither do we...*

29

When Edd Carter pulled up outside his house, he killed his car engine and allowed himself a quiet moment to think back over the afternoon. The Nelsons had been distraught at the thought of their son being taken by some unknown individual. Meanwhile, Edd and Melanie had merely been frustrated, faced down again by the anonymous Michael character that seemed to be popping up and disappearing at uncomfortable speeds. The Michael Richards link had moved from clear to tenuous at best but it had occurred again, and neither Edd nor his DI quite knew how to proceed. The officer sighed hard and rubbed at his face before opening his door and swinging himself out of the car, and that's when he spotted it.

The house was alive with lights and movement – but Emily was meant to be spending the night at her grandmother's house. The thought that something might have happened to his daughter catapulted to the forefront of Edd's mind and he rushed up to the house, fumbled through opening the door, and burst into the hallway – just in time for his blushing smiling daughter to come bounding up to him. Emily launched herself at Edd at such an angle that her head collided with his stomach, and he had to hold in a heave as his daughter clung to him.

Following the fierce concern that something might have harmed her, Edd's relief that Emily was fine washed over him in a crushing wave of gratitude and he knelt down to his daughter's level to kiss her rosy face. But then Trish appeared in the background.

'Mummy's home, did you know? Mummy's home!' Emily delivered the announcement with the same level of excitement that she usually reserved for Christmas morning, in her chorus of 'He's been, he's been' at finding her presents dotted around the living room, and it killed Edd to see his daughter approach her cheating mother with such excitement.

When Edd said nothing, Emily took his hand and guided him toward Trish until the two were just a couple of feet apart. Still holding Edd's hand, Emily reached for Trish's, and with both adults connected through the link of a little girl, Emily announced: 'We're all back together, we're all back to normal!'

Trish shot Edd a smug smile over Emily's head. 'I'm making lasagne for dinner.'

'I already ate,' Edd said, squatting down to Emily's height again. 'Want to show me what you've been doing at school this week?'

'Yes!' Emily replied before dashing around her father and climbing the stairs to fetch her schoolbooks.

Edd was grateful for two minutes alone with his wife. 'You know this is out of order,' he muttered.

'What, coming back to my house?' Trish snapped, more vicious than Edd had expected.

'You don't live here anymore, Trish. You left, remember? You left and gallivanted off.' Edd paused to pull in a deep breath. 'With other men. You abandoned us for a frolic or two with people you barely even bloody know and now what, I'm just supposed to take you back and forget that you've fu–'

'Daddy, I can't find my art book, so I'll have to tell you about maths and English instead.'

'Okay, brainy bean, let's go.' Edd set a hand on his daughter's head as he spoke, feeling her too-soft blonde hair that she'd inherited from her mother. 'I ate at the station, so I'm good for dinner,' Edd told Trish, and he shot her a look as though he were daring her to challenge him on it, but she didn't. Instead, she gave a gentle nod and retreated into the kitchen where, half an hour later, her and Emily would have dinner together while Edd rooted himself to the living room to check through his emails and pay some of the household bills.

After Emily had gone to bed, Trish found Edd in the kitchen, shoving four pieces of bread into the toaster.

'You didn't eat at the station?' she asked from the doorway.

'You know that I didn't.' Edd continued his preparations, pulling butter, cheese and ham out of the fridge as the bread crackled into toast. He flicked the switch on the half-full kettle to set that to boil as he went along. 'Are you going to stand and watch me until this is done?' he asked, turning to face Trish for the first time since she'd appeared. 'I managed to keep myself alive for three weeks, I think I'll be fine for another evening. Unless you've done something to the bread.' He gave her a taut smile as the toast popped up behind him, and Edd turned back to his evening meal preparations.

'Can we talk?' Trish asked.

'No,' Edd said, dragging a buttered knife along the first slice of toast. 'No, we can't.'

'Edd, you're being so–'

'What? What am I being?' He turned to face her, butter knife still in hand. Trish looked taken aback by Edd's tone; he wasn't prone to snapping at her, or raising his voice, but that night he had done both. 'Trish, you can push as hard as you like but you aren't making this go away. You left me, her.' He gestured above his head to where their daughter was sleeping. 'You left both of us without thought or explanation. I had to use my bloody work contacts, and social media of all God-awful things, just to find out where you were. And what if something had happened to Emily? To that girl that you care about so much, and want to come home to?'

Trish opened her mouth to speak but Edd halted her with a raised hand. 'Trish, I don't even want to hear it, whatever it is. You said everything I needed to hear the other night. After that, we're through.' He turned back to finish buttering his toast, but instead sighed heavily and dumped the plate of food into the bin. He paced over to the doorway. 'I'm going upstairs to get blankets. Take the bed. I'll be up early anyway so I'll pack things away before Em gets up.'

'How long can you keep that up for?' Trish asked, moving into his eyeline.

'Until this case is over,' he said, finally looking at her. 'Then we'll make things official.'

Trish didn't push any harder after that. She kept out of the way while Edd searched for blankets and stole the spare pillows from the guest bedroom turned junk room. He made a makeshift bed for himself on the sofa and settled down for the night, taking his phone with him for idle browsing until sleep claimed him. But sleep didn't.

For a good thirty minutes, he could hear Trish shuffling around upstairs as though she were pacing from one side of the bedroom to the other. Half of Edd hoped that she was, that she was plagued by guilt and sadness and it was keeping her awake. More realistically, Edd thought she was likely doing it for some kind of dramatic effect.

It was nearly half past eleven when Trish ceased and, presumably, got into bed. But even then, sleep didn't come easy to Edd.

Despite his best efforts not to, he replayed Trish's explanation from the other evening. The sudden need and want for freedom, for a break from it all, how she explained it away just like that as though it were a normal thing for a wife and mother to do. An uncomfortable blend of anger and confusion swelled in Edd's stomach, forcing him to sit up on the edge of the sofa, taking deep breaths to try to settle his unease. He was almost grateful when his phone flashed up, silently signalling a phone call – until he saw the DI's number displayed.

'Boss?' he answered.

'Did I wake you?' Melanie was quiet, and her lack of urgency made Edd feel more relieved than nervous, which made a change these days.

'No, no, I was up. What do you need?'

'Can you get over to Camden Woods, just behind the playing field where Jenni was found?' The confusion, anger, everything fell from Edd's stomach. He remained seated on the edge of the sofa, bracing himself for what he felt certain was coming. 'We need feet on the ground for this one, Edd. There's another body.'

30

DC Chris Burton felt the frosted grass crunch beneath her. October had brought with it some terrible conditions, and this wasn't the sort of night that anyone wanted to be outside for. Ahead of her in the near distance, she could already see the light show of flashing police vehicles and, the closer she got, she could make out the silhouette of her DI standing in front of a patrol car. Chris closed the remaining distance and stepped over the police tape that had been pinned in place. In her manoeuvre, she spotted Edd Carter treading the same path that she had just come along so she waited, giving her colleague a raised eyebrow expression with a reserved smile as he crossed the cordon.

'Shit's going to hit the fan now, isn't it,' Edd said, his tone flat.

'Come on, let's get it over with.' Chris crossed to greet the DI and Edd followed behind her, their crisp footsteps announcing them enough for Melanie to turn and face them before either detective could offer a greeting.

'Jesus, am I glad to see you,' Melanie said and from the heavy exhale, Chris believed that her superior really was. 'There was a patrol vehicle monitoring the playing fields,' she said, speaking directly to Chris. 'Edd and I thought, after we'd spoken to the

Nelsons, it would be a worthwhile idea to have a PC or two on the ground just in case any kids played silly arses while we weren't looking.'

Chris nodded her understanding. It was a good decision, she thought, one that she would have liked to have been included on – but she tried to let the thought slide. 'They were doing their second lap for the evening, about an hour after their first, when three kids came running out of this clearing.' She pointed behind her. 'They were shouting something about a body.'

A car door slamming closed caught the DI's attention. She cast a look around her and found that the source of the noise was George Waller, closing the door of his unmarked people-carrier. From the outside, no one would know that the vehicle was specially modified to transport bodies from one location to another. Inside, the vehicle was hardly recognisable from its original state.

'Medicine man is here,' she said, stepping away from her colleagues.

'Detective, we must stop meeting like this,' George said, tipping an invisible hat to Melanie. The DI's face remained expressionless; she wasn't quite in the mood for light-heartedness. 'Tough crowd,' George said, more to himself, as he cocked a leg over the cordon and joined Melanie on the investigative side. 'What have we got?'

'Young male, a little frosty around the edges. We haven't moved him but we're ready to.'

'Bag over the head?'

Melanie tutted at her colleague's curtness. 'No, no obvious cause of death that any of us can spot at first glance. We're hoping to find more when we flip him, and when you look at him too.' Melanie held out an arm to gesture to the clearing where the body had been discovered. 'Right this way, doc.'

Melanie nodded for Chris and Edd to follow her. Under normal circumstances they might have tented the body on arrival, but the frost had already gotten to the boy. There were small beads of ice clinging to his spikes of hair, and Melanie couldn't help but flash back to the pinned image of Jenni, Patrick, and Eleanor in their shared happiness – the image of Patrick specifically, with too much gel in his brilliant blond locks. The DI shook away the memory, trying instead to focus on Waller who was down on one knee, pulling on a latex glove.

'Have we called the parents?' Edd asked.

'Not yet,' Melanie replied. 'Not until we're certain.'

Chris and Edd shared a sceptical look. Now they'd seen the body, the detectives thought that there was nothing uncertain about it – but they wouldn't bring themselves to contradict their boss. Instead the DC and DS hovered in the background, overhearing George Waller's preliminary thoughts and findings.

'Young man,' Waller said, rubbing his fingertips over the pale face to dislodge some of the detritus that clung there. 'I'd guess somewhere between fifteen and eighteen, hard to say for definite without thawing him out and having a good look at things.' Waller moved his hands to the boy's neck. Melanie thought he was likely looking for the same, or similar, injuries that had been inflicted on Jenni Grantham. 'It's difficult, you see, because some areas are hardening against this weather.' Waller spoke more to himself than the many officers that surrounded him. 'Professional, preliminary opinion.' He looked pointedly at Melanie to hammer home his meaning and the DI nodded her understanding. 'It's a different method entirely and the boy wasn't strangled or suffocated, which means we're looking for a different something or other here.' Waller scanned over the body as he spoke, looking for obvious injuries or anomalies. 'But there's nothing up front to spot, is there?' he said, agreeing with Melanie's tentative assessment.

'Are we moving him?' Melanie asked.

George appeared to grimace at the suggestion. 'Let me get a bag from the car. I'm not having him flipped here; it'll do more harm than bloody good.'

The ME disappeared, backstepping his way toward his vehicle. Melanie told the surrounding officers to take a breather – 'Thaw your hands out on a car heater or something, we'll need you soon enough.' – giving her a moment of quiet with her DS and her best DC. Chris and Edd both shared a concerned expression, but while Edd made firm eye contact with his boss, Chris looked like she was struggling to pull her eyes away from the young male lying spread on the frosted floor in front of them.

'Burton?' Melanie grabbed her attention.

'Sorry, boss,' Chris said, meeting her senior's look. 'It's just–'

'It's just it looks like Patrick Nelson,' Melanie finished, and Chris couldn't help but let out a gentle sigh of relief that her boss had made this announcement on her own. 'I know it does, Chris. It's important that we get the body with Waller, so he can start countering the effects of the weather, the best he can, at least. Forensics need to be here.' She looked around to check that they weren't. 'We shouldn't be moving the body without them, but I don't see that we have a choice, given the state of things. Nathan Vaughan is the first response for their team.' Melanie nodded towards a man just three feet from the officers who was peeling away a protective layer of department-approved plastic. 'He's taken as much as he can while we were waiting for everyone to arrive.'

'Surely he'll need samples from under the body?' Edd chimed in.

'You'd think so.' Melanie saw George Waller making his way back over to them and she shouted at the resting officers, encouraging them to make their way back to their original standpoint. 'Edd, will you lift?'

Carter threw a nervous look at the boy on the floor and gave his senior a reluctant nod. Meanwhile, George Waller was flattening out the body bag, underneath which he'd already placed an additional layer of plastic sheeting. *That'll please forensics*, Melanie thought. When the plastics were in place and the officers were properly gloved up, six pairs of latex-covered hands reached towards the body to find a part that they could comfortably hold.

'For the love of God,' Waller snapped. 'Don't drag him. We need him clear of the floor entirely, lifted over, and gently placed inside the black plastic covering. Does everyone understand?' While his tone was a touch patronising, Melanie was glad to see the ME taking the situation so seriously. It wasn't always his way, often preferring to make light of things where he could, but perhaps even Waller had his limits. 'Ready on three,' the ME continued. 'One.' The officers tightened their grips. 'Two.' They bent their knees, ready to lift. 'Three.' They heaved the body a clear four inches off the ground, grunts of surprise and discomfort moving around the group as the weight of a lifeless individual dawned on them. 'Now, into the black lining.' The men followed the instruction and when Waller had zipped up the black casing that would carry the boy to the lab, he carefully folded the underneath layer of plastic around the body bag and, reaching for a clip stashed in his back pocket, Waller tacked the edges together in the centre like a small gathering of filo pastry – an unsavoury filling inside.

Without instruction this time, the same group gathered around the body again and lifted, carrying the boy over broken bark and discarded litter, over the cordon of police tape, and eventually into the back of Waller's ready and waiting vehicle. Waller was only just strapping in the body when Nathan headed toward the new scene.

'Mind if I get started?' he asked Melanie who nodded approval.

'Please do,' she said. 'Are the others likely to join you?'

Nathan let out a curt laugh. 'When they're ready,' he said, as he zipped up his second protective suit of the evening. 'I'll need a couple of officers to fetch and carry various bits, if you don't mind? But I'll try to work quickly.'

Melanie headed toward the congregation of officers who were loitering around George Waller's vehicle, but she noticed that Edd wasn't among them. She scanned the area and spotted her DS leaning over the cordon to address a small herd of journalists who had appeared, seemingly out of nowhere – as was their way, Melanie thought. 'How do they get here so fucking fast?' she asked, pulling Chris's attention to the cameras and questions that Edd was fencing. 'Okay, Edd has put himself on press duty which means that we'll–'

'DI Watton?' the shout came from somewhere behind her and Melanie bolted, with Chris close behind her.

There was a small mobile light angled at a patch of ground that had, not too long ago, been underneath the body. Nathan was staring at a sample of something smeared across a small glass plate, his eyes narrowed at the discovery. He lowered his glasses toward the end of his nose and looked up at Melanie:

'Your ME is looking for a head wound. This small pool.' He pointed toward the discoloured patch that he'd illuminated. 'Looks to me like a lot of blood.'

31

Melanie had grabbed at the opportunity to try for an hour of sleep in her office before the team arrived. After everything that had happened, she hadn't bothered going home; she already knew that sleep would evade her there. Instead she had watched while the body was taken away by George Waller to be deposited at his lab for a rushed autopsy in the morning. 'It'll go to the top of my list,' he'd said. And she watched as Nathan and eventually one or two other forensics experts picked at and bagged up the area that had surrounded the boy. By the time they had finished, Melanie was helping them to carry five bags of evidence over to Nathan's car.

'Do you really need all of this?' she asked Nathan, who shrugged.

'It's better to be safe,' he replied, pulling down the boot of his black Corsa. 'I heard what George said, about bumping this to the top of the pile. There's only so much I can do in terms of what everyone else is working on, but I'll personally do what I can over the next few hours.' He flashed Melanie a taut smile before climbing into his vehicle and driving out and away from the woodland.

Since then she had passed the hours checking and double-checking information, reading and rereading files, and napping, her neck cricked at an awkward angle against the back of her desk chair.

She had been half and half when her desk phone howled and pulled her fully into wakefulness. She snatched at the handset and mumbled, 'DI Watton.'

'Are you coming down for this?' George Waller asked.

Melanie took a quick look at her watch. Seven forty-five in the morning, which meant that the team would be arriving any minute – assuming one or two of them weren't already out there. She rubbed at her forehead and ran her tongue around her teeth, which felt coated with the morning fuzziness that always originated from nowhere.

'Can you give me half an hour?' she asked. 'I need to brief people.'

'Thirty minutes and I start, okay, Mel? It's a busy day here.'

Melanie thanked her colleague and disconnected the call. In the bottom drawer of her desk she kept her essentials, which consisted of make-up – for the mornings when she absolutely needed it – and a clean shirt, among one or two other priceless items. She quickly whipped out a pale blue shirt and changed into it, before giving her eyes a lick of mascara in the hope that it would at least detract from the bags beneath them. She took two deep breaths to steady herself before pulling open her office door and, while many of her team – complete with their own tired eyes and weary expressions – were waiting for her, there was an unexpected visitor standing in the centre of the office space as well.

'Mr Nelson,' Melanie said, her hand outstretched as she walked toward him.

'Detective,' he replied, reciprocating the gesture to shake hands. 'I understand you're all very busy.' He seemed to be addressing the room rather than Melanie in particular. 'But I was wondering whether I might have a chat with you, about the boy, in the woodlands?' His voice quivered the further he got into his request; pushed on by a furious wave of sympathy, Melanie found herself standing next to the man in order to guide him by the elbow into her office. It had been a day since she'd seen him, but Mr Nelson looked as though he'd aged beyond his years in that time.

'Please, Mr Nelson, take a seat,' she said, closing the office door behind them.

'It's Philip,' he replied. 'Phil, if you like. Or Philip is fine.'

Melanie sat opposite him and flashed a quick smile. 'What can I do for you, Philip?'

'It's him, isn't it?' he asked, and Melanie's heart sank. The detective wasn't sure what facial expression she'd pulled but whatever it was spurred the man on further. 'I don't mean to put you in an awkward spot, but Rachel and I, we watch the news, and we weren't sleeping, and we saw in the early hours that there was a boy and we thought, God, you know what we thought, and we both said we'd wait and I said I'd get a paper but I ended up here...' His voice trailed off, cracking with emotion in the final words.

'Philip,' Melanie said, making a conscious effort to steady her voice. 'We don't know, that's the honest truth of it, and it's also the reason why we hadn't contacted you and your wife yet. The body that we found is currently with the Medical Examiner who will hopefully tell us more about what happened, and once that's done we'll be able to arrange an identification.'

The tired man opposite Melanie let out a laboured sigh. 'How long will that take?'

'I'm meant to be with him in the next twenty minutes or so, so I can be there when he starts,' she explained, double-checking her watch. 'I promise you, you and your wife will be the first people contacted when these early preliminaries are out of the way. Until then the best thing you can do is stick together and avoid the news,' she said with a soft smile, but it didn't spread to her visitor. Mr Nelson stood with the same tired and withered look that he'd walked in with, and Melanie felt foolish for thinking anything she said would change that.

Without a formal goodbye, Mr Nelson walked toward the door of

Melanie's room but, remembering something, turned to face the detective again. 'He has a birthmark.'

'I'm sorry?'

'On his stomach,' he said, gesturing to his own abdomen. 'It's like a thumbprint and it's on his left side, not quite on his ribcage but you'll know it, if you see it.'

'Thank you.' She nodded, and he went on his way then, having turned down her offer of company for the journey out of the station. Melanie deliberately waited long enough for Mr Nelson to have cleared the main office space before she stepped out into it again. When she pushed through her door for the second time, she found her team buried in work already. 'Did I miss anything?' she asked, addressing the room, but it was Burton who answered her.

'Morris and I are on CCTV still, trying to piece together Patrick's whereabouts through the camera feeds to see if we can get a time-line in place for the night he went missing. Read is looking through Michael Richards' notes, on the off chance there's a link somewhere there, and Fairer is hounding forensics.' Melanie glanced over in time to see Fairer give her a quick wave, his desk phone fixed to his ear and a determined tone heavy in his voice for whomever he was speaking to.

Burton continued. 'We've also got a PC or two on standby in case we get a positive ID on it being Patrick Nelson, so we can lift and shift things from his home; laptop, any consoles he might have used to talk to people, that sort of thing, just to get a jump on tech as quickly as we can as well.'

'Where's Carter?' Melanie asked.

'He's not here. Bad traffic, I suppose. So I took point.'

The two women shared a knowing smile. 'Thanks, Burton.'

'Anytime, boss.'

When Melanie pushed open the door to George Waller's examination room – wearing a faded blue overall and a paper mouth-mask – she was five minutes later than their pre-agreed time and, as also agreed, Waller had already started. Melanie had to make a conscious effort not to recoil in horror at the sight of the young man with a newly made rip down his chest, ready for exploration at a later stage in the autopsy process. Meanwhile, Waller continued with his incisions as Melanie approached, looking up at her only when she was a mere foot away from the table.

'You're late,' he said, standing upright and speaking through his mask. 'But I started early, so I guess we're even.' He crossed to the bright yellow bin leaning against the nearest wall and peeled off his bloodied gloves, before depositing them in there, followed by his mask. 'I didn't need to cut him open for cause of death,' Waller announced, crossing the room again to move back to a laptop that sat toward the front of the office.

'It was that obvious?' Melanie asked, following him.

With a few clicks of the mouse, Waller pulled up a series of pictures that were enlarged by a separate computer monitor. At first it was hard to discern what the images were showing, a close up of something that much was obvious, but beyond that Melanie felt as though she were looking at an optical illusion. At certain angles she saw a dip, but at others she didn't, although she was certain there were at least two colours overlapped in the image.

'George, what am I looking at here?'

The ME sighed. 'Blunt force trauma.' He hit the laptop's enter key as he spoke, calling up a whole new sequence of images. This time the screen showed a series of shots on their way out of the zoom in, and picture by picture, Melanie soon saw the back of their victim's head, a small dip in its centre, with dried brown blood laid over his hair. She put a hand to her mouth to hold in an expletive. 'Let it out, Mel, it's fucking ghastly,' George said, cutting the image feed. 'Did forensics collect up the various shit bits that were lying around?'

'They collected samples of everything that was nearby, yes, some things bigger than others.' She followed George across the room as she spoke, heading back toward the examination table. 'Why do you ask?'

'Because I collected these from around the wound,' he said, picking up a small petri dish. He held the container out for Melanie to observe. 'Splinters, they look like to me, although I'll be packaging them up and sending them to forensics, assuming that you don't have any objections.'

'He was hit over the head with wood?'

'Not over. In. Whoever hit him, this thing went right in. There's such a clear dent that I'd say if you could find the wood, you'd match it to his head like a goddamn mould.' George snapped on a pair of clean gloves as he spoke, readying to resume his examination. 'Anyway, early findings and all that. I'll have a full report for your records as soon as I can type it, but unless I find something drastic in here, we'll be sticking with blunt force.'

'Thanks, George, for everything.' But George waved the gratitude away with a whisk of his hand and sent Melanie packing in the direction of the lab door. 'Wait, can I just check something?' she asked.

George looked up from the growing split in the boy's torso. 'Yes?'

Melanie stepped around the opposite side of the table to face the right side and, holding her breath, she took a quick scan of the boy's stomach. It didn't take much finding, standing out against his pale skin like a little neon symbol, the exact size and shape his father had made it out to be – a small but distinct little thumbprint.

32

After everything, Melanie couldn't stand the thought of pulling the Nelsons into Waller's office for the sake of an identification. They deserved to see their child at his best and, given Waller's plans, it would be a while before that option was given to them. So before she had left, Melanie had requested from Waller two pictures: one of the boy's face, and one of the boy's birthmark. It wasn't Waller's first stroll around the block and he understood the DI's plans without her sharing them; so he obliged, angling the young man's head away from the light to try to lessen the cobwebs of colouring that had formed under his freezing skin during his time outside. He handed the pictures over to Melanie and wished her luck before the DI went on her way, stopping at the station to collect DC Burton.

'How sure are we?' Chris asked as she climbed into the car.

'So sure that this is actually just closure,' Melanie replied, pulling away into the flow of traffic. The DI already knew, in her gut, that the young man on Waller's table was Patrick Nelson. It was a case of finalising the identification and finding the sick soul who had murdered another kid. 'Do you think it's the same person, same people?' Melanie asked, riffing off from her own thoughts.

'Yes,' Chris answered without skipping a beat and Melanie shot her a quick look. 'It's too much of a coincidence otherwise. Two kids from the same college who happened to be best friends, killed in the span of two weeks? We're either looking for the same two people who attacked Jenni Grantham, or we're looking for someone sicker than the people who attacked Jenni, and they're just looking to make waves by killing Jenni's friends.' Chris watched as Melanie frowned over option two. 'No, I'm not buying that we've got three psychos in a five-mile radius and this is the first we're hearing of it either. It's the same people, boss, I'm sure of it.'

After this, Melanie's silence stretched out for most of the journey. She needed the time to ready herself for what was coming. As they turned into the Nelsons' road, she finally spoke.

'You'll make a good DS one day, Burton, you know that?' The DI pulled up outside of the Nelsons' house and killed the engine without saying another word on the matter. Meanwhile, Chris was shocked into a delighted silence that she knew she needed to shake before she exited the vehicle. 'Good to go?' Melanie asked, craning for a look at Chris's face. The DC nodded, unbuckled herself from the seat, and stepped out of the car in time with her boss.

They'd barely set a foot on the path leading to the Nelsons' house when the front door opened. Melanie had been expecting Mr Nelson, after his eagerness at the station, but instead it was Mrs Nelson in the doorway, her solemn expression and sad eyes greeting the officers as they arrived on her doorstep. Melanie gave her a thin smile, which the grieving mother reciprocated with some effort.

'It's him, isn't it,' Rachel Nelson asked in a resigned tone. Melanie knew that the parents were braced for this and, not wanting to string their pain out any longer than necessary, she gave the woman a gentle nod. Rachel Nelson sidestepped to let the pair of officers into the house, adding, 'Phil is in the living room,' as they walked by her.

'Mr Nelson,' Melanie said on entering the room and the man,

perched on the edge of the sofa as though about to get up, turned to look at her. His eyes were ringed with red patches and Melanie guessed that there had been tears shed over the last few hours. 'My colleague, DC Burton, and I have some images that we'd like to show you and your wife, if you're both comfortable looking at them.'

Mrs Nelson joined her husband on the sofa as Melanie and Chris took their seats opposite. Rachel gave her husband's knee a gentle squeeze before meeting Melanie's gaze.

'We don't mind, no.'

With the same level of care she imagined someone would take with a real body, Melanie eased the photographs out of their folder slowly. She balanced the image of the birthmark on her palm and handed it over to Mrs Nelson who grabbed it with considerably less care than Melanie had shown. But the mother was eager, desperate even, and Melanie could understand that.

The DI followed this image with the second one showing the boy's face. She held back a wince at the sight of the boy who had become discoloured during his time in the woodlands, hoping that the parents wouldn't notice the telltale signs of a body abandoned outside.

Mr Nelson leaned forward to take this second image and as soon as he clapped eyes on the photograph, he sucked in too much air, which he quickly forced back in a difficult cough. Melanie and Chris shared a nervous glance while both parents assessed their respective images, saying nothing for what felt like the longest time.

Mr Nelson spoke first. 'Oh,' he said, as though remembering their company. When he looked up to speak directly at the officers, Melanie spotted tears clinging to the edges of his eyes, ready to rush down his cheeks at any given blink. 'I'm sorry, officers, I – well, I.' He shook his head lightly, clenched his eyes, and the tears fell. 'I do think it's him, yes.' He passed the image across to his wife, refusing to open his eyes again until the photograph had changed hands. He reached across to the small table standing at the side of the sofa, a box of tissues perched on top, at the ready. Pulling out two, three, four, he dabbed at his own eyes while passing two tissues across to his wife, sensing her need without even looking at her. In these seconds, the room remained so quiet that every one of Mrs Nelson's tears that collided with the printed image landed as a loud dollop.

'It's him,' Mrs Nelson eventually announced to the room and her husband approved her statement with a firm nod. 'Yes, it's definitely him.' She ran a tissue beneath each eye to catch the final tears before handing both images back across to Melanie, who quickly stashed them into the cardboard folder, out of sight. 'Who – who would have done this?' Mrs Nelson asked, her words struggling to fight their way out.

'Is it the same person who got Jenni, is that what you're thinking?' Philip Nelson chimed.

'At the moment, we're unsure,' Melanie said. 'There's an obvious connection between the cases and we can't write this off as sheer coincidence, so moving forward, we will treat them as related incidents until we find a reason to think otherwise.'

'Good God.' Philip Nelson wore an expression of utter confusion. 'I can't make sense – I just can't understand any of this. They're children, nothing more than children, honestly.' He was pleading with the officers, as though either Melanie or Chris might do something to reverse the recent events, and the DI felt helpless in the face of the pleading man. 'Have you told the Granthams?' he eventually asked.

'What about Eleanor?' Mrs Nelson added.

Melanie leapt in. 'What about Eleanor, Mrs Nelson?'

'Is she a target? If they've got Jenni, if they've got – if they've got our Patrick, should Eleanor's parents be worried. Should someone be watching her?'

'We'll have a police car patrolling past Eleanor Gregory's house for the next few days, and we'll be talking to her parents about minding her whereabouts a little more than usual, should there be any risk. Although we don't currently have evidence to suggest that there is,' Chris rattled off her reassurance like a practiced speaker and Melanie was notably impressed with her DC's fast thinking.

'There is evidence though, isn't there?' Mr Nelson pushed. 'There are two bodies. Isn't that evidence?'

'That's not what they mean, Phil.' Mrs Nelson tried to settle her husband. The man shook his head and adopted the same look of confusion from earlier, slipping back into quiet. 'We'd like to see Patrick, as soon as we can, please.'

'I understand. Our Medical Examiner will contact us when his investigations are complete, and we'll be able to arrange a viewing for you both...' Melanie caught sight of Mr Nelson's stunned face and decided to revise her offer. 'Or for just one of you, it's not compulsory that you see him. Either way, we'll arrange things as quickly as we can.'

'When his investigations are complete. Does that mean you don't know what happened?' Mrs Nelson asked, latching on to Melanie's words.

Too many thoughts rushed through Melanie's head at once and she decided, against protocol perhaps, to answer with her gut instead of a guidebook. 'No, at the minute we don't know what happened. But we should know something in the next day or two.'

The Nelsons thanked the officers for their time – although neither women felt like they deserved the parents' gratitude – and they declined the offer of a Family Liaison Officer. 'We don't need someone rattling around the house with us,' Mrs Nelson had said and Melanie, unwilling to fight a grieving parent, had let the issue go.

The DI and DC were midway through their journey back to the station, with a heavy silence sitting between them in the car. Chris couldn't decide whether it was the weight of their visit as a whole, or whether it was one thing in particular that was troubling her boss...

'I would have lied about Waller's preliminaries too,' the DC said, guessing at the trouble. The heavy silence held its place for a second or two longer before Melanie eventually replied.

'Thanks, Chris, that's actually good to know.'

33

Superintendent Archer arranged for a press conference, featuring both DI Melanie Watton and DI Thomas Williams from the Missing Persons department. Melanie gave an eye roll at the mention of Missing Persons' involvement, but Archer made her case – 'They've got a fair bit to answer for.' – and no more was said on the matter. It took two days to arrange for the right journalists and media to be involved, now their humble home-ground case had caught the attention of the bigger-named papers.

'I've heard The Daily Mail will be there,' Fairer said as he flicked through his computer's controls, trying to find the right website for live-streamed television.

'Why do you think that's exciting?' Burton replied, her tone one of genuine curiosity.

Elsewhere in the station, Melanie was sitting across a table from Edd Carter, talking strategies on what to reveal and what not to reveal. The pair had been talking for nearly half an hour and had decided that Melanie needed to be as vague as possible, giving out very few specific details on Patrick's death to avoid tipping off anyone who might be involved – or rather, anyone trying to be involved. With the newly applied pressure sitting firmly on the team to crack the case, they were eager to weed out the false witnesses before they got into full bloom, and limiting the public details was the best way of doing that. The two were about to pick up another strand of their discussion when a firm knock came at the door.

'Come in,' Melanie shouted, and in walked Superintendent Archer, donned in her most formal attire with a troubled look on her face. Both officers immediately stood to attention, somewhat startled by the appearance of their superior. 'Ma'am, apologies, I didn't realise that you were going to be around for this.'

'Around?' Archer repeated. 'I'm making up part of the panel.'

Melanie and Edd swapped a look. 'Are things that bad?' the DS asked.

Archer sighed. 'We've got two dead kids in as many weeks, Carter, things certainly aren't good.' She shot a pointed look at Melanie. 'Are you ready?'

Carter excused himself and allowed the two women some privacy to walk to the press room on their own. They did so in silence, neither in the right frame of mind to make small talk with the other.

When they were outside the press room, all either officer could muster was a thin smile, quickly tucked away as they stepped in to face the pack of interrogators waiting for them. Melanie had never seen the room so fit to bursting with press officials and, for the first time in her career, she knew hardly anyone in the room. It occurred to her then just how big the case was becoming, the defining one of her career even, a thought that terrified and excited her in equal measure, although it did nothing for her concerns about being able to catch their killer – killers, however many they were looking for.

The superintendent and the DI took their seats at the table, and while bulbs flashed and journalists readied themselves for the opening of questions, the two officers present waited for the arrival of the third. As Archer checked her watch for the second time, DI Williams fell through the door with a blank expression and a dishevelled appearance that set Melanie's eyes rolling again, and she hoped that the cameras hadn't caught her.

'Now we're all present and accounted for,' Superintendent Archer started. 'We have invited you here this afternoon to discuss the developments in the Jenni Grantham case, tied, it seems, to the Patrick Nelson case as well. You are all of course aware of the restrictions around what we can and cannot reveal as part of the ongoing investigation, but nevertheless we invite you to ask questions and I, and my officers, will answer them to the best of our abilities. Before that, it will help you to know where we currently are with our investigations.'

Archer relayed a potted version of both cases that Melanie had provided for her the day before, although the superintendent recited the details as though she'd done the groundwork on each case herself, such was her confidence and assuredness.

As her overview came to an end, the superior officer opened up the opportunity for questions, of which there appeared to be many.

'Superintendent Archer, you implied earlier that the two murders are tied, what exactly do you mean by that?' The first question came from a young gentleman at the back of the room who was dressed for a job interview, his tie so tight that it looked as though it were pinching his neck. By comparison to the local journalists that Melanie was accustomed to dealing with, the young man might well have been the most professional member of the press Melanie had seen.

'DI Watton may be able to tell you more about that.'

Melanie swallowed hard and the gulp echoed from the microphone in front of her. 'At the moment, we're assuming there is a link between the two cases, but we cannot currently confirm what that link may be. As we've said, it's very early days in both investigations, particularly in Patrick Nelson's, where we are still waiting for a final autopsy report before making any definite conclusions.'

'So they weren't killed in the same way?' The question came from a more familiar face this time. Melanie's head snapped round to catch sight of Heather Shawly, her pen poised ready for an answer.

'I'm afraid we can't release that information yet,' Melanie replied.

Heather pushed again. 'Presumably, if you can't directly tie them together, then–'

Superintendent Archer cut across the woman with a swiftness that would have made Melanie smile with glee – under other circumstances. 'It's a little busy in here, Ms Shawly, I think one question per journalist is fair for the time being.' Heather Shawly had a bad reputation for being a hard and harsh wordsmith, and Melanie thought it couldn't come soon enough for someone to take the woman down a peg. Archer shifted her gaze. 'May we have a question from this side of the room?'

'What involvement have Missing Persons had with this case exactly?' The question came from another new face and it was expertly avoided by Archer, who redirected the query to an uncomfortable-looking DI Williams. Melanie leaned forward to hear the DI's spin on his involvement. Whatever was coming, she thought, it better be good...

Fairer continued to click through buttons on his computer, trying but failing several times over to find the right feed for the press conference.

'Why don't we just go down and stand in on it? It's free viewing in real life too,' Read said, standing from his seat as he spoke.

'The DI doesn't want us there, said she doesn't want us yanked into things,' Burton answered, her attention half-pulled away from her colleague as the door to the office opened and Carter came wandering in through it. 'How was she?' Chris asked.

Edd sighed. 'As you'd expect.'

'Wait,' Lucy Morris snapped. 'Wait, Brian, go back a click.'

'What did you spot?' Fairer asked, following the order.

But as he backclicked, there was no explanation necessary. It wasn't quite the press conference, but something just as eye opening. An image of Mrs Gregory sitting alongside her daughter, Eleanor, filled the screen with a news banner across the bottom that read: *The second wave of Michael Richards*. The Gregorys had been told to keep their heads down, out of protection for their child more so than anything else, but it looked as though they hadn't heeded the advice. Edd leaned forward and hit the volume button on the computer's keyboard, allowing Eleanor's voice to fill the room.

'It's terrifying... like the thought someone's out there targeting kids my age, people I know. We've never done anything to anyone, you know? We don't deserve this.'

'You're so right, and you're so young to feel so threatened,' the newscaster replied, her voice false and encouraging. 'How's it been for you? You mentioned earlier that you'd been asked by the local police to keep a low profile for the time being, that can't be easy for a young woman of your age.'

'So easy that she hasn't managed to do it,' Read chimed in and there was a murmur of agreement around the room.

'It seems unreasonable,' Mrs Gregory pitched in. 'Asking a girl of her age to stay off the grid. I mean, they should be getting the killer off the grid, not our children.'

'I just feel like I can't do anything without worrying that whoever got my friends might be out there, watching me,' Eleanor said, lowering her head as though she were crying, although when she looked back to the newscaster, her eyes showed no signs of it. 'I'm locked in my home to avoid some, some – well, some nutter.' The young woman turned to her mother, shielding her face entirely. The camera lingered on them both for a second before spinning to focus on the newscaster, prompting Fairer to cut the feed to the programme.

'Bloody brilliant.' Carter sighed.

Chris rubbed hard at her eyes in a frustrated gesture. 'Some nutter, she says, locked in her home, she says. Glad she isn't giving that nutter a map to where she's hiding.'

34

Melanie had left her office door open, so when she slammed down her desk phone with an almighty clatter, it called in the attention of her officers working outside. She was aware of their eyes on her but she couldn't bring herself to care, due to her frustration following yet another phone call with Mrs Gregory. The mother had decided that there was money to be made from her daughter's current press status – although she hadn't openly admitted the monetary motivations.

But the DI had seen enough of Gregory's type around in her years to know the reasons behind their influx of television appearances. For the last twenty-four hours, it had felt to Melanie like she couldn't turn on a news report without seeing Eleanor Gregory's face – or, on the few occasions when it hadn't been Eleanor, it had been one of her dead friends instead, which wasn't exactly preferable. But the girl's mother couldn't be reasoned with, and despite the potential threat to her daughter, Mrs Gregory's opinions clearly wouldn't change.

With a hard sigh, Melanie balanced her elbows on the edge of her desk and dropped her head into her hands, the pressure in her forehead already building into something that would no doubt be another headache before the day was out.

Chris Burton stood just outside of Melanie's office as she reached in to tap on the door. 'Got a minute?' Melanie sighed but gestured to the chair opposite her, and Chris came to sit down. 'What's going on your end?' the DC asked, noting her boss's worsening mood.

'We have no idea who this killer is, and Mrs Gregory is parading her daughter about like a prize trophy for having not been targeted yet. I just think...' Melanie broke off, revising her comment. 'You would think that both of them, Eleanor included, would be more safety conscious, instead of lapping up the attention like it's, like it's just a game, like this isn't dangerous.' Melanie felt herself losing track of her sentence, so she held up a hand as though physically pausing herself. 'This isn't what you're here for,' she said. 'What do you need?'

Chris half-stood to lay out a series of grainy images across her boss's desk before dropping herself back into the chair behind her. Melanie leaned forward, taking stock of the photographs that she quickly realised were camera stills, showing their most recent victim, Patrick Nelson, dotted around in different locations.

'Lucy and I have been scouring the CCTV footage that was sent in by various businesses, companies, you name it. We might not be able to tell you why Patrick Nelson ended up at the woodland, but we can tell you that he followed this route to get there and that he changed course halfway through his route, after taking a phone call.'

'How do you know he took a phone call?' Melanie asked, peering up from the display.

Chris leaned forward and tapped a finger on the fifth image from the left. 'Because we've got him doing it on camera.' Melanie took a closer look at the image Chris was pointing to and spotted the change in Patrick's stance; he wasn't mid-walk but rather still at an angle that made him look like he was facing a street, with his hand pressed to his ear. 'After this, he back tracked along these same streets again, because we picked him up twice on some of the cameras, and changed direction entirely, heading toward the woodland instead.'

'Okay, gimme a rundown of his route,' Melanie said, leaning back.

'We first pick him up on Milburn Street, outside of Jack's Shack, and the next time we see him is around five minutes after that outside of the Tesco Extra on Western Road,' Chris said, pointing to each image as she spoke. 'We can track him through Wilson's Mills, Merrygate Way, and that's when he takes the phone call, standing outside a cash point at Carlton Stop. After all of this, he back tracks half the distance but turns onto Pickerway Park, and that's when we lose him for a good twelve minutes before he appears, one last time, on the old industrial estate.'

'Which is a shortcut to the woodland,' Melanie concluded.

'Exactly.'

'Is there any way of working out where he was heading originally, before the phone call?'

Chris frowned. 'We've tried, but it's way too broad without more footage, which we could apply for, if need be, but the route he was originally taking would have led to the college, and it would have also led to Jenni's house, Eleanor's house, the Breezewall shopping centre. There's no way of knowing for certain, I don't think.'

'And there's no trace on his phone still?' Melanie asked.

Chris shook her head. 'No, but Lucy is over with the tech team now because they've finally got Patrick's laptop from his parents, so they'll be cracking into that any minute, and Lucy said she'd report back to us assuming they find something of interest.'

'They have to,' Melanie replied.

'Why?'

'Firstly, we need them to, for the sake of the case. Secondly, if we're assuming the same killers are responsible for both Jenni and Patrick, then there's every reason to think that "Michael Richards", whoever they may be, will have contacted Patrick the same way they did Jenni, via the Internet.'

Another knock at the open door pulled Melanie's attention up from her conversation. There was a constable standing in her doorway, holding a brown A4 envelope.

'I'm sorry to interrupt, DI Watton, but a courier has just dropped this off at the front desk. I believe it's from the forensics department,' he said. Melanie gestured him into the office proper and he handed over the envelope as though it were made from a precious metal. Melanie could only hope that its contents would be so valuable.

'Thanks for this,' the DI said, already ripping into the paperwork as the officer exited the room. Chris kept quiet while her senior read through the contents of the delivery. Midway through the second sheet of paper, Melanie's eyebrows pulled together, and her forehead creased into a deep frown. 'This can't be right.'

'What can't?' Chris asked, edging forward.

'There's the obvious stuff. The splinters in Patrick's head, that George sent over, well they were definitely splinters, and they can be matched to the surrounding wood, so we know the blunt force trauma theory is likely correct, unless George finds something else. But they've...' Melanie petered out, mouthing the words on the paper in front of her, but not allowing them to materialise into sound. 'Sorry, Chris, this is hard work. Patrick's DNA has been put into the system and it's flagged up a match.'

Chris hesitated. 'I don't understand, boss, what kind of match?'

Melanie set the paper down, her frown still fixed in place. 'Patrick's DNA is a match to the male sample that was found on Jenni Grantham's body.'

35

D S Edd Carter gathered his team into the centre of the office, in front of the packed-to-bursting evidence board. Perfectly timed, Melanie walked in just moments after the detectives' shuffle had settled. She'd called ahead on her journey back from the forensics lab and asked Edd to ensure that everyone was present and accounted for, and to ensure there was no one else within earshot outside of their office space. Inside, the DI closed the door behind her, peered through the window glass to give one last check over the corridor outside, and then pressed in the small lock on the end of the door handle, before heading to stand at the front of the room.

'What I'm about to tell you doesn't leave this office,' she said, sending a wave of concerned looks from one officer to the next. 'Forensics sent over a messenger earlier with results of their latest DNA results. When Patrick Nelson's DNA was put into the system, it flagged up a match with Jenni Grantham's body.' The sound of intrigue and confusion followed but Melanie pressed on, the time for questions was much later. 'I've been over there just now to try to identify exactly what this means for Patrick's involvement in Jenni's murder. It turns out the DNA was found at different points on Jenni's clothing, which doesn't really have much of an impact over Patrick's reputation, but his DNA was also found on the bag and the tie that was round Jenni's neck.'

'Oh, Jesus,' came from somewhere at the back of the huddle.

'Obviously, this evidence is a little harder to ignore. We're not drawing any conclusions yet, but a working theory seems to be that whoever Patrick was with when Jenni died may have turned on Patrick in the end, killing him, and bringing us to this point. It's the only solid idea that we've got to work on. I'd like evidence for and against as soon as anyone can provide it.' She paused in her speech to perch on the edge of a nearby desk before addressing her team again. 'So where are we, kids. What do we actually know?'

'Boss, sorry, back up. We're thinking Patrick murdered Jenni?' David Read piped up.

'Do you have another suggestion?' Melanie replied, her tone flat.

'And what about the DNA on Patrick, where are we with that?' Carter added.

'Forensics are trying to match it, somehow, to the other samples that were found on Jenni. They're hoping that there might be enough in this new sample to expand on the original DNA. If so, they'll be able to put a profile together for us. But they're ifs and buts for the time being and frankly, forensics are being good to us here, so I'm not about to bust them up for further details before they're ready. They've said it'll be tomorrow at the earliest if they get something,' Melanie said with a shrug before looking over her whole team again, desperate for someone to have something.

Lucy Morris raised a nervous hand.

'Morris?' Melanie obliged.

'I've got a thing,' she muttered. 'I think.' The DC headed over to her workstation and pulled up something on the computer screen, shielded from the officers behind her. It was a few seconds later when the interactive board – sleek and stark in contrast to the cluttered evidence board next to it – kicked into life and showed an expanded view of the DC's desktop. 'We've been going over Patrick's conversation history. There are some things between him and Jenni, which we'll get to, but there was also this...' Morris double-clicked a small icon and a string of conversations unfolded in front of the detectives.

TheRealMichaelRichards:
    Did she seemed worried though

'Michael, our old friend,' Carter said, leaning forward to get a better view. The detectives around him, Watton included, had their attentions fixed to the board while Morris recited the conversation aloud.

GiveMeNelson:
    Not worried no
    If anything she seems excited
    Which makes me feel bad

TheRealMichaelRichards:
    Bad
    Why
    We've been planning this
    She understands how it'll work

GiveMeNelson:
    Does she though

Morris turned to face her colleagues, leaving a short sample of the conversation suspended in front of them. 'CliffsNotes,' she said. 'In the minutes after this they talk about "her" and "she" a lot, without going as far to name anyone, so we don't actually have Jenni's name on record. However, we do have a lot of messages that show Patrick as being complicit in whatever this plan is that they're talking about.' Lucy turned to scroll into a new chunk of the conversation thread before turning back to face the room again. 'This is about the worst of it.'

TheRealMichaelRichards:
    She won't make anything of her life without this Paddy
    We're giving her something to die for
    See what I did there
    Think about how many people will know her after this
    How many people will know us

Lucy left this snippet suspended on the screen as she addressed the group. 'This conversation, along with some of the conversations that Patrick shared with Jenni, were hidden on the laptop in the same way that Jenni's conversations were. Again, given Patrick's inability to even clear his own search history–'

'Wait, what's so bad about his search history?' Fairer interrupted.

'Nothing, by a teenage boy's standards,' Morris replied, cutting her colleague quiet. 'Given that that had never been cleared out, it seems unlikely that he was in the habit of organising covert conversations without someone guiding him to it.'

'This is good stuff, Morris, nicely done,' Melanie said, still inspecting the same message splayed over the board. 'There's more?'

'There is,' Lucy replied, turning to orchestrate another series of clicks. Several conversation windows unfolded across the screen, creating a layered effect. 'There are quite a few between Patrick and

Jenni, but this is one of the more interesting ones, two days before Jenni died.'

GiveMeNelson:

    Are you feeling okay about the plans for Halloween

JenniGRR:

    A bit nervous still

    But it'll be a good laugh won't it

    And it'll shit my parents up

GiveMeNelson:

    Aren't you a bit more worried

    I mean, this is pretty major

    We just want you to be sure

    Jen you still there

JenniGRR:

    Has MR said something to you

    Like they don't think I'll go through with it

    Because I'll go through with it alright

Melanie read through the remains of the conversation which talked around the same subject matter, and she simply couldn't make sense of it. Did Jenni know what was about to happen to her? Worse still, did she help her attackers orchestrate it? Melanie looked around her team and saw confusion mirrored back from them and, while it in part comforted her to know their state was a shared one, she'd been hoping that one of them would at least have something to offer.

'The conversations between the two victims have been printed,' Morris said, picking up a pile of stapled stacks of paper from the edge of her desk. 'I took it upon myself to give you some homework for the night.'

'Look at you, acting the detective,' Burton said, playful but gentle.

'About time,' Fairer piped up.

'And what have you found today, Brian?' Melanie snapped, silencing the DC and commanding the attention of the room again. 'No one takes these documents home with them. It's great to have them, Lucy,' she said, not wanting to discourage the young officer from showing initiative. 'But they can't leave the office, not with how things are. If you're reading, then you're staying here. Carter,' she called her DS's attention up from the transcripts he was already scanning through. 'First thing tomorrow, we're going to pull Eleanor Gregory in.'

'From college?' he asked.

Melanie shook her head. 'Her mother is keeping her out of school, something about being able to ensure her safety at home.' There was a curt laugh from someone and when Melanie scanned the room for its source, she found Chris, her hand clasped to her mouth.

36

Melanie Watton and Edd Carter stood outside the front door of the Gregorys' house, meanwhile Chris Burton was across town talking to the Granthams, with David Read in tow. Both sets of detectives had their separate mission statements. Chris was primarily interested in knowing about Jenni's boyfriends, girlfriends, any romantic entanglements she'd had in her young life.

Over the course of the previous evening's thought-shower sessions, Melanie and the team had decided that whoever The Real Michael Richards was, it must have been someone who Jenni trusted – and there was no one that a young woman trusted more than her first love. On the other side of town, Melanie was grilling Eleanor for Michael Richards information too – but she was more concerned about whether the Gregory girl had her own entanglements with the mystical figure.

Mrs Gregory pulled open the door and immediately stepped to one side to allow the detectives through. They had called ahead to ensure that neither mother nor daughter were otherwise engaged – with a television or radio interview, Melanie had thought, but not said, during the phone conversation with the stern mother. On more than one occasion, Melanie had even wondered whether Mother

Gregory might have had something to do with this whole shit show herself. The detective had brushed away the suspicions each time but, given the continuously frosty receptions that the officers were receiving, it was hard not to suspect the woman of something.

Melanie stepped through the doorway into the living room where Eleanor was sitting, interview ready, it seemed. The girl was perched on the edge of the sofa, legs crossed, and hands folded in her lap as though her mother had coached her through constructing the right appearance. But whatever the desired effect of it was, Melanie was more perturbed than she was impressed. The DI sat on the sofa opposite the girl and Edd soon joined her, followed by Mrs Gregory who merely lingered in the background, reluctant to take a seat next to her daughter, but equally reluctant to let the girl speak for herself too much either.

'Do you mind if we record this?' Melanie asked, retrieving a Dictaphone from the inside pocket of her suit jacket. 'We would have preferred you down at the station, Eleanor, but your mother said you weren't quite feeling up to it.' Melanie leaned forward to set the device on the table between them both but kept her eyes level with Eleanor long enough to see the girl shoot her mother a cutting look. 'We can always go to the station if you'd prefer. We can certainly handle the mob outside.'

Melanie and Edd had pushed through a handful of journalists to get to the front door, but they'd given them space enough as soon as Melanie threatened a temporary restraint on their work. The DI was confident that if they could get in then they could certainly get the girl out, but even Eleanor dismissed the idea this time.

'It's okay. Mum thinks it safer for me, being at home and all.' Her voice was steady, less excited than Melanie had heard it in interviews. 'What is it that you need help with?'

'Frankly, Eleanor, we're finding out some interesting information between Patrick and Jenni's computers, and I'm starting to find it hard to believe that you don't know at least something of what was going on with them, between them,' Melanie said, her tone level but not accusing; she genuinely sounded curious.

Eleanor and her mother were clearly taken aback by the question though. 'What are you implying, Detective In–?'

'I'm not implying anything, Mrs Gregory,' Melanie cut across the woman. 'I'm outright asking Eleanor what her involvement is with this case, because there is an involvement, isn't there?' She looked pointedly at the teenager who stared back, unflinching. 'Do you know who killed your friends?'

Eleanor stretched her eyes wide at the suggestion. 'Hang on, *that's* what you think I know?' she blurted, and Melanie felt relieved to have at least got what appeared to be an authentic reaction. 'You think I'd keep quiet about who killed them. Are you for real?'

'You're being absurd, detectives, bloody absurd,' Mrs Gregory snapped. 'Is this the point that your dead ends have brought you to?'

Melanie ignored the mother's interruption and continued. 'Okay, well if that's not what you know, what do you know?'

Eleanor rolled her eyes and let out a huff. 'Jesus, I know Jenni was mad on Patrick, okay? She was mad on him and she would have done anything that he asked her to, that's what I know.' She dropped against the back of the sofa and held eye contact with Melanie for a beat before swapping her look to Edd. Neither officer spoke though, holding the silence until it became uncomfortable. 'What, you think there's more?'

'Is there not?' Edd picked up.

'There genuinely isn't, I swear. She had a soft spot for Patrick and he had a soft spot for serial killers, so she played dress up like he asked her to, and that's as much as I know. I don't know why she was researching Michael Richards, or who the Michael Richards she was talking to online was, and I certainly haven't spoken to the weirdo.' The words were rushed, a panicked response from a teenager in way over her head, Melanie wondered, but there was something about the girl that still didn't sit right.

Edd shot a look at Mrs Gregory. 'Whoever this is, he, she, they're targeting the kids through a fake messenger profile. If you're interested in keeping your daughter safe, I'd consider restricting her Internet access for a while.' He stood as he spoke, angling his eyeline to look down on the woman. 'Parent to parent, this is. I'm not speaking as a detective.' Now he was upright, Edd had better access to his inside pocket and from it he retrieved a small plastic bag with a sealed DNA swab kit inside, which he passed to Melanie.

'You're going to take a DNA sample?' Eleanor asked as the DI unzipped the kit.

'If you and your mother have no objections,' Melanie replied.

But of course, Mrs Gregory did. 'Why do you need one?'

'Eliminations more so than anything. We've taken a lot of samples from Jenni and Patrick but given the amount of time the three of you spent together...' Melanie was splitting her explanation between mother and daughter, looking from one to the other as she spoke. 'It's no surprise that we'd find a lot of your DNA on their clothing and that sort of thing. It'll just make life easier all round.' This seemed to pacify Mrs Gregory, but Melanie wanted to be sure that she had the teenager on board. 'Are you sure you're okay with this?' she spoke to the young woman directly.

Eleanor flashed a smile that bordered close to a smirk. 'I'm relieved that you've asked.' She threw her mouth wide open like a child readying for a sweet to be thrown at her, and Melanie carefully rubbed the swab along the inside of the girl's cheek before packaging it back into its protective gear. 'So that'll be on record now?' Eleanor asked.

'Once the lab has processed it, yep,' Edd explained as the DI took great care to ensure the swab was properly sealed before slipping it into her own inside pocket. With that item safely stashed away, she picked up the recording device that had lain with its lights blinking between her and the girl. She hit pause, then stop, before killing the power and pocketing the small machine.

With only a hint of sarcasm, Carter thanked Mrs Gregory for her help in the ongoing investigations while Melanie gave Eleanor a sincerer note of thanks before standing. The officers excused themselves, assuring Mrs Gregory that it wasn't necessary for her to see them off the premises, and they held their pensive silence until they were a good four paces down the driveway, heading back toward their vehicle.

'What are your thoughts, Edd?' Melanie asked, eyeing her colleague from the side.

'Honestly, boss, I don't have much to add about her revelation. They're a group of teenagers. I would have been more surprised if one of them didn't fancy the other.' He paused to unlock the car and walked around to the driver's side. Speaking over the top of the vehicle, he added: 'What I did find interesting was Eleanor's comment about not knowing who The Real Michael Richards is, from the chats between them and Jenni.'

'You find it interesting that she claims not to know who it is?'

'No, no,' Edd continued. 'I find it interesting she knows about The Real Michael Richards screen name, given that I never told her that's who Jenni was talking to.'

37

It was the morning after when the team as a whole could reconvene from their respective duties. Melanie had brought breakfast – bacon and egg sandwiches for everyone – but it was clear that nearly three weeks of eighteen-hour days was starting to take its toll on them all, the DI included. She hoped that a new discovery would boost team morale, but it seemed unlikely that anything was going to come their way. Fairer had looked into the names that Gibbons had listed as potential troublemakers, but none of them showed any real cause for concern.

'They're just bloody kids, aren't they? Gibbons' idea of what a troublemaker is, is a far cry from ours.'

Meanwhile, Burton and Read didn't have much luck with their avenues for enquiry either. They had spent a portion of the afternoon asking the Granthams for details of their daughter's romantic life, but it seemed that this was another empty avenue.

'They said she never really showed an interest in boys,' Read explained.

'Or girls,' Chris added, noting Melanie's raised eyebrow. 'They said that at one point they wondered whether Jenni and Patrick were likely to become a thing, but it was clear that there was nothing there after they saw them together. Close friends, both parents agreed. We managed to make it over to the Nelson house as well,' Chris said, looking down at a small strip of paper balanced on her thigh. 'We've got one or two names of girls, mostly from the college. It looks as though Patrick wasn't shy about bringing people home with him, but neither of his parents thought there was really anyone of note within all this.'

Melanie eased off the edge of the desk where she'd been balanced and ran a hand through her messed hair. 'There must be something here,' she said, turning to face the evidence board. 'What are we missing?'

'What about Eleanor?' Chris asked, pulling back the DI's attention.

'Oh, she's a delight,' the DI replied, sitting down to address the room. 'She told us that Jenni and Patrick were a thing, but we've got no evidence for that. She also told us she didn't know who The Real Michael Richards is, which Carter found particularly interesting, given...'

'I never told her the screen name of who Jenni was talking to,' Edd completed his boss's opening. 'We took a DNA swab, which she seemed far too fucking cheery about as well.'

'Long and short, she knows more than she's willing to tell us still,' Melanie finished.

'Can't we drag her in?' Read piped up. 'Surely that's what we'd normally do.'

'On what grounds?' Melanie asked, with genuine hope that her DC might suggest something.

'Withholding evidence?' Chris suggested.

'Obstructing a police investigation?'

A wave of suggestions moved around the room and, while Melanie admired the stirrings of optimism that were shifting through the team, she was yet to hear anything that she could use to justifiably bring Eleanor in for cautioned questioning.

'We'll keep pushing. Whatever's there, we'll find it. She's a teenage girl. How many of those do you know who can keep a secret on a permanent basis?' Melanie said, silencing the suggestions that were still mid-flow. 'Morris, any luck with Waller?'

Lucy pulled up a sheet of A4 paper that had been lying on her lap and read. 'Patrick Nelson died from blunt force trauma to the back of the head. There were at least three separate blows delivered, as determined from the angles of the wound. The approximate time of death is three days before his discovery.' She looked up to address the room. 'Which confirms that he was never abducted, incidentally, he was killed on the night he went missing.' She looked down to continue reading. 'There were pressure marks and bruising around his neck, as though someone had started to strangle him but ceased, and there was DNA found around these markings sent to the lab for further testing.' Morris paused again to address the DI. 'That's the stuff that forensics is trying to match to Jenni's unknown sample.' She set the paper down. 'That's everything really. Waller said he'd email you a full report but that's the highlight reel.'

'Is there any way to tell which blow killed him?' Chris Burton asked.

Morris looked over the sheet. 'Not that I've got listed here, no.'

'Why do you ask?' the DI replied.

'I'm wondering whether it's a clumsy kill or whether it's someone going to town on their victim,' Chris explained. 'If the first blow killed him, the second two will have just been anger.'

Edd let out a long stream of air as he rubbed his eyes. 'I don't know what's worse.'

The hours after were spent revisiting the evidence they already had, while chasing up the evidence they'd yet to receive. Melanie cautioned the team against rushing DNA testing, but Fairer and Read were sent on their merry way for an update of general forensics found at the scene of Patrick's murder. The remaining officers walked each other through their independent discoveries and made patchwork quilts of them over the course of the day, trying time and again to find a workable – and, more importantly, provable – theory.

By the time Melanie came up for air and checked her watch, the team had worked well into early evening.

'Christ, you all have homes to go to,' she said, standing up from their new collaborative space; a paper-littered table in the centre of the room. 'If you have any major breakthroughs, sleep through them and tell me in the morning,' she half-joked, moving toward her office. Once inside, she packed as much paperwork as she could into her briefcase. It might be time to go home, she thought, but it wasn't time to stop working.

'If you need a hand...'

Melanie looked up to find Carter and Burton standing in her doorway, both officers wearing expectant expressions. The DI smiled. 'It's a lovely offer, but what about Trish?' she directed the question to Edd before turning to Chris. 'And poor Joe?'

'Please, a takeaway without me glaring in judgement? Joe'll love it,' Chris replied. The two women shared a smile before turning to Edd, ready to hear his excuse.

He rubbed at the back of his neck and let out a half-laugh, but the noise sounded awkward and forced. 'Things aren't great at home,' he said, not meeting the eyes of either women as he spoke, but Mel and Chris shared a private concerned look.

'It's unprofessional to hug,' Mel said, a half-laugh emerging. 'But are you okay?'

Edd shrugged. 'I've been better.' He took a deep breath and announced, 'Trish went on a bender, slept with a few blokes, took the joint account. Emily and I were on our own for about two weeks. Now Trish is back, and things are even harder.' He poured the news out onto the floor of Melanie's office, unable to hold the look of either of his colleagues.

Chris silently reached across and set a hand on her colleague's arm, pulling his attention up to her. 'I'm sorry,' she said, and he flashed a thin smile.

Melanie heaved her packed workbag up from on top of her desk. She wanted to offer him comfort, to be a friend, but inside the station, she knew that their boundaries were clear. 'We're a sad lot, aren't we,' she said to break the silence and the group managed to share a laugh. 'So, party at my house? I've got a fine selection of Chinese takeaways on offer.'

The many evidence files that Melanie had smuggled home with her were spread out across her living room carpet, her fellow officers positioned around them, forming a triangle with her. They'd been jumping between images and documents for what felt like hours, and Edd was glad when the front doorbell sounded to signal the arrival of their dinner. The DS was the first up and off the floor, crossing the living room and darting through the doorway.

'I'll get food,' he shouted back.

'I'll get plates,' Chris said, and smiled at the DI who was still rapt with the image she was holding. The commotion of food arriving hadn't disturbed Melanie, but the squeal of her mobile phone, ringing from somewhere inside her coat pocket, was enough to grab her attention.

'I'll get that,' she said, noticing for the first time that the room was empty. She retrieved the handset from her coat, carelessly draped over the back of a dining room chair. *Private Number* was branded across the screen, so the DI pulled herself back into professional mode to answer. 'DI Watton.'

'Hi there, it's Kelly, Kelly O'Brien, from the forensics department.' Melanie checked her watch. It was nearly eight in the evening. 'I know it's late,' the caller continued. 'But I was left with strict instructions to call you if something were to come back from the tests we're running here and, well, something did.'

Melanie sat down on the closest sofa. 'Thanks for calling, Kelly. What do you know?'

'The sample from the first and second murder, we were running a comparative analysis on them to see whether they were from the same donor, but obviously the first sample we had wasn't substantial. Anyway, look, I'm not going into the science of it...' Melanie felt a stab of gratitude. 'But we managed to match them, the first and second DNA donation are from the same person, and we've profiled it back as belonging to a female.'

Melanie grabbed at a piece of paper and wrote down. *Female accomplice?*

'Jesus, okay, thank you for calling with this,' the DI replied but the expert at the other end of the line picked up speaking again.

'There's more. Once we'd cleared up the sample, we ran it through the system to see if it pulled any matches.' Melanie's heartbeat was audible in her ears, the adrenalin, the sheer thought of a break in the case left the DI holding her breath in the hope that this was going where she expected it to.

'Can you repeat that, please,' Melanie asked, her excitement waylaying her understanding.

This time Kelly spoke slowly, clearly. 'I said, we got a match.'

38

Eleanor Gregory sat alone in a well-lit interview room, her eyes tired from lack of sleep, and her neck cricked from a night hunched up on what passed for a bed inside a police cell. Her mother had ardently protested the whole thing, but in the end Eleanor had gone willingly, holding her wrists behind her back as though eager for Melanie to place the handcuffs on her.

Eleanor had been transported to the station the previous evening where she had been detained on grounds of being a danger to those around her. Being suspected of two murders in as many weeks seemed to convince the chief superintendent that exceptions could be made for this particular case.

Two storeys above the interview room, Melanie and her team were working furiously to process the new information that was coming at them in violent waves. Morris, with the help of the technology team and an eager Chris, was working through the contents of Eleanor's laptop. Elsewhere, Carter was reading and documenting messages and call logs from the suspect's phone. There had been bagged up items of clothing wedged in the back of Eleanor's wardrobe that the officers also found in the early hours of the morning, and DCs Fairer and Read had couriered those over to forensics where they were currently waiting for all and any results the team might be able to find at short notice. The entire office was working in full throttle and for the first time since this charade began, Melanie finally felt as though the team had a measure of control.

The DI checked her watch and, noting the time as just after eight fifteen, she headed down to the main reception in the hope that their requested social services worker might be there by now. She broke into a run on her way down, suddenly desperate to do everything in as fast a time as possible, as though making up for the previous weeks. But when she pushed through the doors into the main reception, far from finding a new face, Melanie was greeted with an all-too-familiar one.

'Where is she?' Mrs Gregory spat, rising from her seat and closing the gap between herself and the DI at a speed. 'You've had her all night, you should be done with her now.'

'Mrs Gregory, I'm afraid we haven't even started. There's a lot of evidence to proce–'

'Evidence?' the woman repeated, in a notably higher pitch. 'Surely, as you've bloody arrested her, you should have all your bloody evidence.' Each word landed with a physical weight that Melanie fought against reacting to. Instead she took a small step back, lengthening the gap between her and the other woman, and tried to explain.

'We have enough evidence to hold her, Mrs Gregory, but we're now in possession of certain items that will help to determine Eleanor's involvement in this whole thing.' Mrs Gregory parted her lips to speak but Melanie pressed on. 'If you really want to help Eleanor, then perhaps you'll agree to an interview yourself.'

The woman appeared taken aback. 'Why on earth would you want an interview with me?'

'To determine *your* involvement in this whole thing,' Melanie said with a smile that she couldn't stifle. 'You're under no obligation, of course, and perhaps you'd like a solicitor to accompany you and advise you, which is also understandable.'

The more Melanie explained, the more offended the woman appeared.

'This is ridiculous, Detective Inspector, utterly ridiculous. Do you suppose that I killed them now? Is that your new theory?' The woman shook her head at the thought. 'I've no need for a solicitor, as I've done nothing wrong, but if it helps to clear up this bloody madness then of course I'll agree to an interview, as soon as you're ready and able,' she said, implying that Melanie was not either at present.

Melanie crossed the room to speak to the sergeant behind the desk. 'Are there any interview rooms free at the moment?'

The man glanced down to a small display, hidden behind the counter. 'Interview room three appears to be empty, Detective, if that's of any use.'

'Marvellous,' Melanie replied. She turned to face a newly startled-looking Mrs Gregory. 'Shall we?'

Melanie led the woman down a light grey corridor and into a room that was sparsely decorated; the only furniture it boasted was a table and four chairs, strategically placed in the centre of the space.

'Please, do sit,' Melanie offered, taking a seat herself. Mrs Gregory pulled out a chair on the opposite side of the table. 'There's recording equipment fitted throughout the room so, for the benefit of the recording, could you please confirm your name?'

'Fiona Gregory,' the woman announced, with more hesitation than the act called for.

'And I am Detective Inspector Melanie Watton.' Melanie knew that she was running wild with this interview, but she also knew that an uninhibited conversation with the suspect's mother might not come around again too soon. Melanie also knew that she'd have to carefully play the cards that they held, and feel her way forward from there. The detective pulled in a deep breath to steady herself before she began. 'Mrs Gregory, I'm not going to ask you for hard facts because it hardly seems fair given the rushed nature of this interview,' Melanie said, deliberately softening her tone. 'But I would like to know some more details of your daughter's character, as you know her, that might go some way toward determining what's really happened here. Does that sound okay to you, Mrs Gregory?'

'Of course,' the woman agreed, although she didn't sound certain.

'Okay. How would you describe your daughter?' Melanie tried to start with a relatively easy question, but Mrs Gregory pulled her eyebrows together by way of responding to it. 'On a day-to-day basis,' Melanie tried to clarify. 'Is she lively, friendly, helpful?'

'All of those things.' Melanie felt as though Mrs Gregory had thrown herself on the answers, trying to catch each positive description of her daughter before it became hidden by something less savoury. 'She's always helping around the house, she does very well with everything at college, and–'

'Actually, we have a testimony from Mr Gibbons, who has branded Eleanor as a bit of a troublemaker from time to time. Is this news to you?' Melanie asked, and from the expression spreading across the other woman's face, the detective knew that this reveal wasn't exactly a surprise. 'So, she's prone to being a bit of a troublemaker?'

Mrs Gregory rolled her eyes. 'A little, yes, I suppose. But she's a teenager, she's no more or less of a troublemaker than her friends.'

'Her dead friends?' Melanie asked, her tone flat and her expression sceptical.

'Detective–'

'You're quite right, Mrs Gregory, that was unfair of me. But speaking of her friends, what were your thoughts on Jenni Grantham and Patrick Nelson, were they troublemakers?'

Mrs Gregory seemed to consider this for longer than she had done previous questions. 'They could be, all children can be, but generally they always seemed very well behaved to me. Patrick could be boisterous, I know, but Jenni was always, she was always very kind.' Mrs Gregory's voice had taken on a note of sadness at the mention of Jenni, her eyes watering suddenly. 'It's a sad business, what's happened to those children.'

'And you firmly believe that your daughter had nothing to do with it?'

Mrs Gregory stood up in a rush, knocking the table as she did. 'Detective, I will not sit here, and have you talk about my daughter like she's a bloody murderer, when I know full well that she is not. She's not perfect, no–'

'Why did you parade her around, Mrs Gregory? Can we talk about that for a moment?' The subject change startled the woman and Melanie couldn't help but push at it a touch harder. 'Why did you let her on every television and radio segment that asked? Was that for yourself or for your daughter?'

Thrown, the woman sank back into her seat. She rested her elbows on the table in front of her and cradled her head in her hands, avoiding eye contact with the detective. 'Because she asked,' she said, in a quiet voice. 'Because Eleanor asked and begged, and I couldn't say no because everything around her was terrible and this was something good, or something she thought would be good and I just, I wanted something good out of it all.'

For the first time, Melanie felt a stab of sympathy for the woman. The DI and her team had assumed that it had all been the mother's doing, that Mrs Gregory was the driving force behind the interviews, the showmanship, when all along it had been Eleanor. Although, sad as Mrs Gregory looked, Melanie couldn't help but feel pleased with this latest revelation, as credence, further evidence toward the type of young woman they were readying to face off against, just two interview rooms away.

'Mrs Gregory,' Melanie continued, readying for one final blow. 'Our forensics experts have found Eleanor's DNA on both Jenni

Grantham and Patrick Nelson, in places where only the killer's DNA would be found.'

'I don't understand...'

'Eleanor's DNA was found underneath the bag that was wrapped around Jenni Grantham's neck, and larger traces of it have since been found–'

'DI Watton.' Superintendent Archer spoke in a raised tone as the door opened with a force that sent it slamming back into the wall behind it. 'A word, if you please.'

39

Superintendent Archer's face was a pale red, but it was blooming into something much fiercer as she waited for the corridor to clear. Melanie knew that she was in for a reprimand, but she was grateful that her superior at least planned to do it in private. As the last police constable trailed away following a burglary suspect, Archer turned to face Melanie square on.

'What are you playing at, dragging that woman in there without counsel?'

'She didn't want any,' Melanie replied, pleased that she had this truth in her armoury.

'And where's your supporting detective? Carter, Burton? Do either of them know that you're in here, or did you go in unprotected with the mother of a suspected murderer?' Melanie was shot quiet on this one. Like a rumbled child, her eyes darted everywhere but in the direction of her accuser, and her guilt was all too obvious. 'I thought as much,' Archer continued. 'Your social services worker is here to act as Eleanor Gregory's appropriate adult, and the duty solicitor has arrived. I gave permission for both of them to have an hour with the girl before formal interviews begin.'

Melanie let out a light sigh. 'Thank you, Ma'am.'

'Yes, well,' Archer replied, seemingly uncomfortable. 'This has eaten into that hour, I'm afraid, so if I were you I'd get upstairs and get an interview plan together sharpish.'

'But what about–'

'I'll see that the formalities are properly explained to Mrs Gregory from here on,' the superintendent said, cutting across her junior officer, and Melanie had no inclination to fight with her on this. The DI knew that she'd gotten away lightly, as reprimands from Archer went.

Melanie thanked her superior – still not quite making eye contact – and excused herself, before bounding up the stairs two at a time to get back in the company of her team.

When she pushed through into MIT's central office space, she stepped into a hive of activity. Her team barely noticed she was back, they were so busy carrying one lot of evidence to one person, trading it for another, finding something else worth checking out on their way back to their desks. Worker bees turned superheroes, Melanie could see that she hadn't been the only one trying to make up for lost time. She scanned the room for Carter and, spotting him mid-conversation with Burton, Melanie waved them both toward her.

'We need interview strategies, kids, I've got thirty minutes before I need to be in with Eleanor Gregory,' Melanie said, taking a seat at a nearby table. The DS and DC swapped a smug look, still standing in front their superior. 'What, what did I miss?'

'Slow and steady strategy. You ask her about her Internet habits, how reliant she is on her phone, maybe how good she thinks she is with computers. But the main part of the interview should be when you hit her with this.' Edd punctuated his speech by throwing a cardboard folder down on the desk in front of Melanie, the contents of which were spilling out due to the sheer volume of them.

'What's this, Edd? What are you giving me here?'

There was another shared look between the two junior officers. Chris threw a glance at the clock pinned to the wall and said, 'Get reading, you've got twenty-five minutes to learn as much as you can.'

Melanie and Edd stepped into the interview room upholding a formal silence. Around the centre table there sat Eleanor Gregory, her new social worker – Izzy Hughes, as Melanie had been informed – and the duty solicitor, who Melanie recognised as Oliver Lane. Oliver was seated alongside Eleanor while Izzy had pushed her seat back from the table, excluding herself from the conversation but still making her presence known. Melanie and Edd took their seats opposite the suspect and her legal representative, and Melanie formally started the interview.

'I am DI Melanie Watton, and this is my colleague DS Edd Carter. For the purpose of this interview recording, could you please state your names.'

'Oliver Lane, duty solicitor,' the man replied.

'Eleanor Gregory.'

Even now, when she was tired, when she was caught, the girl didn't sound downtrodden and she certainly didn't look like she felt guilty. Edd was sure that he saw the beginnings of a smile when he and Melanie had walked into the room, and he hoped that the surveillance had caught it too.

'We'd like to talk to you about your Internet habits, Eleanor,' Melanie said, shuffling the paperwork in front of her while ensuring it stayed hidden from the suspect.

'What about them?' Eleanor replied.

'Would you say that you're an active Internet user?'

The girl snorted out a puff of air. 'Course. I'm seventeen.'

'And you use it for what, general social media updates, browsing, that sort of thing?'

'I guess, and homework, sometimes.'

'Ah, so you use it for research?'

Eleanor shifted in her seat. 'Yeah, when I need to do research for college.'

'So, I'm assuming that...' Melanie picked up a sheet of paper and read directly from it. '*Manual strangulation* is something that you needed to research for college reasons?' She looked over the sheet of paper to eye Eleanor, but the girl was still giving nothing away, so the DI continued. 'What about, *top ten murderers uk*, was that a college thing?'

'It might have been, I can't–'

'How about *hiding conversations on laptop*, does that one sound familiar?' Melanie cut across her and Oliver Lane leapt in before Eleanor could reply.

'Detective, the two areas seem unrelated to me. Is there some connective tissue here?'

'Funny you should ask.' Melanie turned around the sheet of paper that she'd been reading from to present it to the solicitor and his client. 'This is a list of search terms that we pulled from your laptop, although it took a while, given the jiggery pokery that we had to do to get into the thing.' Melanie paused and eyed Eleanor. This time Mel was sure the young woman was sitting on a smug smile. 'It's not a comprehensive list but just some highlights, and we've managed to time and date them all. Here.' Melanie tapped a side column on the page. 'These different terms, how to hide conversations, how to manually strangle someone, and the others you can see listed there, they build a timeline of our case.'

'What do you mean?' Eleanor replied.

'I mean, two weeks after you looked up how to hide online conversations, Jenni and Patrick started to have secret conversations with a screen name we couldn't trace, for example. Or...' Melanie peered over to look at the sheet. 'How about how you researched manual strangulation a week before Jenni died.'

'Is there a question here?' Oliver asked.

'Yes. Can you explain that timeline, Eleanor?'

The teenager shared a look with her solicitor before facing Melanie. 'Not really.'

Melanie sifted out another sheet from the pile in front of her. 'Okay,' she said, facing another strip of paper toward the suspect. 'Can you maybe explain why you've googled *Jenni Grantham* thirty-two times in the space of two weeks, all since her murder?'

'I was looking for something,' Eleanor replied.

'What? Details on the case?'

The girl released another puff of air, shook her head, and smiled. 'No, DI Watton, not details on the case.'

Melanie wasn't sure whether it was hearing the girl use her formal title, or whether it was her overall tone, but something about Eleanor Gregory's persona appeared to shift with that one answer, and Melanie felt spurred on to push at the girl even harder.

'We've established that you're an active Internet user, how about your mobile phone?' Melanie asked, swapping a look with Edd who pulled out a sheet of paper from his own interview pack.

'Again, I'm a teenager, so...'

Edd read from the sheet in front of him. 'You can't balls out of this now, Paddy. We've done it and there's no undoing it.' Edd read again before looking over the sheet. 'Should I continue?' When no answer came from Eleanor, Edd read another text. 'Meet me and we'll talk about this.' He set the paper down. 'Those messages were sent the night that Patrick Nelson went missing; the night that we know now, Patrick Nelson was murdered.'

Melanie wasn't sure, but she thought Oliver Lane had just allowed a slight shake of his head. She wondered whether the full weight of the case was dawning on the tired solicitor.

'Shortly after these messages,' Edd continued. 'It looks as though you made a call to Patrick, which lasted around a minute. What was the nature of that call?'

'I was telling him where to meet me,' Eleanor replied.

Melanie felt a pull in her stomach, triggered by the girl's unashamed honesty. 'And where were you telling him to meet you?'

'Don't answer that, Eleanor.'

'I want to answer,' Eleanor said, turning to look directly at her solicitor before facing Melanie again. 'I was telling him to meet me at the woodlands.'

Oliver Lane let out a stifled breath. Meanwhile, Izzy Hughes, tucked away in the corner, looked too stunned to say anything at all.

'Is that a confession?' Edd asked, leaning forward.

Eleanor almost laughed. 'What else do you have in that folder?' she asked, directing the question at Melanie rather than Edd, but not waiting for a response from either of them. 'You must have found the clothes by now.'

Without skipping a beat, Melanie replied, 'The ones in the back of your wardrobe?'

'They're the ones.'

'Eleanor.' Izzy had finally come around. 'Eleanor, I think it's best if we take a break.'

'I concur,' Oliver chimed in. 'It's been a long night and a tired morning, Eleanor doesn't know what she's agreeing to or not agreeing to here.'

'No, no I do,' the teenager spoke directly to her defenders. 'You've found the clothes, but I don't think you'll have had time to test them yet, right? Even if you rushed it, they still wouldn't be done by now.' She looked from Melanie to Edd and back again, as though waiting for a response this time. 'So, you've got laptop, phone, written plans, clothes,' she counted off each item along her fingers as she spoke, measured and calm but somehow childlike. Cool as Melanie had been throughout the interview so far, she was disturbed by the sight of their suspect relaying the evidence against herself so readily.

'Eleanor.' Melanie sat forward, closing some of the distance between her and the young woman. 'You need to be really careful with how you answer this question, and I would consider listening to your counsel before you commit to anything.' She shot Oliver a look as a friendly warning for what was coming next, but Melanie couldn't hold off any longer. 'Are you formally confessing to the murders of Jenni Grantham and Patrick Nelson?'

'Eleanor, don't–'

'Stop telling me what to do,' she snapped at Oliver and the demanding child that Mrs Gregory had described just two hours earlier was all too clear to Melanie in those seconds.

When Eleanor looked at the DI again, the young woman's face was pulled into a clear smirk, and as she spoke there was a slight laugh bubbling beneath the surface: 'Why do you need a confession?' the girl asked. She nodded toward the stuffed file sitting between her and the detective inspector. 'Look how easy I've already made it for you.'

40

The rest of the team stood still in the viewing area, watching the details unfold before their eyes. Midway through the proceedings, Superintendent Archer entered and joined in the viewing, maintaining a stern silence until Melanie and Edd had exited the interview space. When the feed to the room was cut, the entire group seemed to exhale in unison.

'What the fuck was that?' Read exclaimed, his eyes widening as he turned to see his superior standing at the back. 'Ma'am, my apologies, I didn't–'

'Don't apologise, Read. I'd say your sentiment was quite right.' The shock lay heavy throughout the room until the superintendent gave instructions to stir the group into action. 'Surely we should head back toward the incident room. There are things to discuss here.' She turned to exit with a trail of confused detectives following in her wake. The collective was halfway back to the room when they stumbled upon Melanie and Edd, both detectives leaning back against the wall of an empty corridor. Melanie chugged at a can of Coke while Edd took up the reigns of addressing the team.

'Ma'am.' He nodded, standing upright from his leaning post. 'I suppose the rest of your saw that display?'

Chris acted as spokesperson for the group. 'All of it. Are you both okay?'

Melanie looked up. 'Shocked, relieved, a little sick.'

'That sounds about right,' Archer intervened. 'Let's get you back to your base so you can regroup. We need to get this wrapped up as soon as possible. A break for everyone, then I want you back in.'

'As early as this afternoon?' Melanie asked.

'She's feeling talkative, Watton, and there's more we need to know.'

'Like what? She killed them,' Fairer piped up.

'So it seems,' Archer replied. 'But I want to know why.'

The superintendent continued to pave the way back to the office and stayed with the team of detectives until they were seated and settled. Speaking quietly to Melanie, Archer explained her exit – 'Things need to be in place for when this goes public.' – before leaving the team to strategise. The detectives seemed to revolve around Melanie and Edd, as though sensing that their first ninety minutes with the suspect had drained a significant measure of energy from them. After two cans of Coke, Melanie felt a little more with the situation, but she was still grateful to those around her for picking up the baton. The team continued to collaborate on theories; Fairer was convinced it was a teenage love triangle while Read remained optimistic that the young woman had been coerced.

'She's just a kid,' the DC argued.

'Even kids can be bad,' Burton replied, deliberately avoiding eye contact with Edd. He was the only member of the team to have a kid waiting for him at the end of every day; the case might hit him even harder because of that. 'What's your take on it, boss?' Chris asked Melanie, drawing the DI back into the conversation.

Melanie thought, not for the first time, how she could possibly answer that question. A second or two had passed when she ventured, 'I think she wanted to get caught. I just don't understand why.'

. . .

Eleanor had eaten two sandwiches and managed half an hour of sleep since Melanie and Edd had last seen her, and the difference that made was clear. The teenager was bright eyed, straight-backed and all ears as soon as Melanie formally started the interview. Before entering the room, the detectives had it on Izzy Hughes' authority that, despite being given the option not to continue, Eleanor was as eager to speak to the police as they were to speak to her. Although the thought of more twisted logic upset Melanie's stomach, the DI knew that she had to wade through whatever was coming if she stood any chance of her and her team emerging victorious on the other side of this investigation.

'Eleanor, why did you google Jenni's name so many times after her death?' Melanie asked. There was a page full of notes splayed out in front of the detective should she need prompting, but Melanie already had a clear idea of where she wanted this discussion to go.

'To see how many hits there were.'

'To see how popular her name was, you mean?' Melanie asked, and Eleanor nodded. 'Is that the same reason why you googled Michael Richards before and after Jenni's murder?'

Again, Eleanor nodded. 'When he died, a year ago or whatever it was, he was everywhere again. That's how I found out about the murders. He was so popular, so known, and I knew that Jenni would get people talking about him again–'

'Eleanor, I'm advising you against continuing with this,' Oliver Lane cut in, but the girl continued speaking all the same.

'So, I wanted to know how much of a difference it would make.'

Melanie frowned. 'Is that why you all arranged it?'

'What do you mean?'

'Eleanor,' Oliver tried again, and the teenager threw him a look. 'You're digging your own grave here,' he spoke quietly, lowering his voice to address just the girl.

'And you're wasting your time,' Eleanor replied, before turning back to Melanie. The DI waited for final interventions, but Oliver was – or at least looked – defeated by his client, so she continued.

'Maybe I'm leaping ahead here,' the DI said, still trying to contain her eagerness. 'The three of you wanted to know what difference it would make, that's what you're saying?'

'Patrick and I did, yeah. But how would Jenni know?'

Melanie took in a quick pull of air, quietly planning a tactic change. 'What involvement did Jenni have with all this?'

'She didn't have anything to do with it.'

'But in yours and Patrick's messages to her, you were all planning something?'

'A Halloween prank,' the teenager replied. She answered each question without hesitation, ignoring every attempt at an interruption that her solicitor made, instead powering through in helping the police piece together their discoveries. Melanie wondered whether this was strategic, whether Eleanor was hoping for brownie points for having helped the police when it really counted. But something told the detective that the young woman was more interested in other end results.

'That's what you were discussing in your messages, under the Michael Richards moniker? It was all just meant to be a prank?'

Eleanor sighed. 'We were getting her to dress up like a Michael Richards victim, and we were going to stage the murder but as like, art, or something. Like an interactive thing where people would find her on the playing fields. That's what she thought; that's what we told her.'

'But all along you and Patrick were planning to kill her?'

'Patrick didn't do much,' Eleanor announced, with something that sounded a little too much like pride. 'He was meant to, but he wasn't great with stuff, really.'

'Talk me through the night that Jenni died, would you? It wasn't meant to happen until Halloween?' Melanie pushed.

'Detective Inspector, do you not think this is unfair?' Oliver Lane intervened.

'Can I wave my right to counsel?' Eleanor asked, throwing a pointed look at the solicitor.

'We're both here to help you, Eleanor,' Izzy added from her corner of the room.

'If Eleanor's happy to continue being interviewed, she's not distressed or uncomfortable, then I'm happy to continue interviewing her,' Melanie said, looking at both Oliver Lane and Izzy Hughes in turn.

'I'm happy,' the teenager chimed with a smile that made Edd wince. 'Jenni thought everything was happening on Halloween, but we planned it out differently. We were going to do a practice, we'd decided that already, and on the night it happened, before we, you know, we'd told her just to treat the whole thing like a run through.'

Melanie thought for a second. 'That's why when she was stopped at the pub–'

'She was acting panicked, like she had somewhere to be?' Eleanor filled in. 'We told her to go to the playing fields to see what it was like at that time of night, but we were there already when she arrived. Patrick grabbed her from behind, but he couldn't do it right,' Eleanor said with a hint of judgement in her voice. Edd shifted uncomfortably in his seat but Melanie was determined to work through this reveal, now they'd finally arrived at it.

'So, you strangled her?' the DI asked.

Eleanor looked at Oliver who, with wide eyes, shot her a firm shake of the head, but the teenager continued all the same: 'I killed her. Patrick just helped with the staging.'

She said it all so easily, as though talking someone through a school project, scene by scene. Melanie swallowed down a bubbling feeling of disgust that was spreading through her lower abdomen; in part, she was facing down a deeply confused minor, but she was uncomfortably aware that she was also facing down a cold and calculated murderer. The detective took a breath to steady herself before asking the next question.

'And what was Patrick's murder meant to achieve?'

Eleanor narrowed her eyes. It was the first question that seemed to throw her off balance. There hadn't been any searches for Patrick's name in the days after his death, so he already didn't fit the pattern of Jenni's murder. But Melanie thought there must be a reason to explain Patrick's murder away – in Eleanor's mind at least.

When the teenager spoke again, it was slowly, as though addressing a child. 'Patrick and I were meant to get caught together. He wanted to duck out on me. That's what it achieved.'

'What do you mean, meant to get caught?' Edd stepped in, unable to stop himself.

'Jesus, did you work out anything?' Eleanor snapped with a tone that Melanie thought the girl probably used with her mother. The DI felt a sudden urge to apologise to Mrs Gregory for all of the incorrect judgements she'd made about the woman. 'Patrick didn't think you'd work it out. He genuinely thought, after like, a week, that we were safe from you guys. He called me to say we shouldn't say anything, we should keep quiet and let it all fizzle out. And I couldn't go along with that, not after all the work and the planning. That's why I met him that night.'

'That's why you killed him,' Melanie said, completing the narrative, and Eleanor smiled.

'I genuinely didn't plan that one though,' the girl said, leaning forward as though addressing Melanie privately. 'He thought we could just let Jenni be a cold case, after everything, *everything* that I'd done to make all of this happen. I was so angry, and he was just ready to walk away, and I couldn't let that happen, you know, not after everything, Detective. I couldn't not get caught, after everything.'

'That's why you left so much evidence everywhere.' Again, Eleanor smiled and this time nodded. But Melanie couldn't understand it all. The pieces were laid out so clearly but none of it made sense. Why would anyone want this? Why would any teenager throw their life away, for what? 'Eleanor, you're going to have to help me out here,' the DI said, admitting defeat. If Eleanor was so eager to explain everything to them, maybe there was one last explanation that she'd be happy to share. 'Why would you do all of this, orchestrate all of this?'

Eleanor smiled and looked in turn from one adult to the next, until her eyes settled on Melanie again. 'Have you googled me yet?'

41

The incident room was hollow. The desks were empty, and the computers were powered down, the evidence board half-dismantled, with only the essential details left for ease of access when the team wrote up their final notes. Melanie sat in quiet solitude, her office door open but her blinds angled to keep out the winter sun. She hadn't been able to settle at home. After three weeks of non-stop investigative work, winding down for some quiet solitude seemed impossible, especially when there was still so much work to be done.

Once the interview had drawn to a close, Melanie had taken it upon herself to visit Mrs Gregory, who had collapsed in a mound of tears on hearing what her own daughter had confessed to. The woman's tone had changed from how Melanie remembered it, as though the detective's announcement had softened her – or maybe broken her.

'You're absolutely sure?' Mrs Gregory asked, looking up from her crouched position on the sofa. 'She couldn't be lying?' The desperation in the mother's voice hit Melanie with a force but, despite wanting to offer her comfort, the DI knew that there was little she could give.

'Even without the confession, we've got enough evidence,' Melanie explained, before trying to give the mother some guidance on what would happen next. She explained how the court case would, should go, if everything went to plan, and gave Mrs Gregory a rough timeline of events from here to sentencing – including when, and how often, she would be able to see her daughter during that time, assuming that she wanted to. Mrs Gregory didn't offer anything by way of a response to the thought of seeing her child though. By the end of their talk, Melanie wasn't sure how much information the woman had taken in, but at least the DI could leave knowing that she'd tried, that she'd done something, no matter how small.

Mrs Gregory wasn't the hardest of the trips though. After discussing Eleanor's detainment with her mother, Melanie went back to the station to collect Burton.

'We'll take the Granthams,' Melanie said to Carter. 'Can you take the Nelsons? Take Morris with you, would you? She could use some time away from screens.'

Melanie and Chris sat with the Granthams to explain their discoveries, the evidence, and the confession. Both detectives had expected questions but there hadn't been many at all. Robert Grantham wanted to know whether Eleanor would be punished, meanwhile Evie wanted to know how long for, but their questions petered out after that. 'If you think of anything...' Melanie reminded them as she and Chris stood to leave, but neither parent seemed to be listening anymore. The couple had turned into each other, seeking solace in their depleted unit, forever missing their third, integral, piece.

The detective inspector had called the team in for a morning debrief, now the parents, press and everyone else was aware of the break in the case. But as the team had ploughed through their piles of paperwork, Melanie dismissed them. She reasoned that they easily deserved a half-day skive with all the extra hours from the last few weeks anyway, and she followed their lead out of the station.

The DI had managed a full two hours at home before coming back to the office to start work on her final report, which she was already three pages into. It had been such a hard and unexpected case, Melanie knew that it wouldn't be out of her system until Eleanor was sentenced and the victims were buried. Although she hated the word, after something like this, closure was the final necessity for everyone involved.

Melanie's head was hidden behind her desk as she searched through filed documents in a nearby drawer, when she became aware of a change in the lighting – as though someone had stepped across her doorway. Her head shot up and she found Carter and Burton looking in at her, and the three detectives again shared a half-laugh.

'You can't settle at home either?' Chris asked.

Melanie exhaled heavily. 'No chance, it seems.'

'Us neither,' Edd added. 'We thought we'd get a jump on things here.'

'Might as well make ourselves useful,' Chris chimed in.

Melanie admired their determination and, not for the first time over the last few weeks, she felt honoured to work alongside such committed individuals – even DCs Read and Fairer had proven their weight during the Eleanor Gregory case, Melanie thought, although she decided to keep her initial reservations about the two to herself.

'I hear Oliver Lane is blowing a fuse about representing Eleanor,' Edd said, stepping into the office and dropping himself into the chair opposite Melanie's.

'Can you blame him?' the DI replied.

'It's going to be a rough one. There's no doubting that she did it, is there.'

'Like I told Mrs Gregory, even without the confession, Eleanor left enough evidence lying around for us to put a strong case together. Plus, whether the confession stays in the police transcripts or not, I think Lane will have a hard time convincing the girl not to confess again,' Melanie answered.

Chris followed Edd's lead and crossed the boundary into the office, coming to a stop behind her seated colleague. 'They'll try her as an adult, won't they? Diminished capacity, though?' the DC asked, her tone somewhat worried.

Melanie shrugged. 'Unfortunately, that's not our job, Burton.'

Chris gave her boss a thin smile and Edd reached behind him to give his colleague a squeeze on the hand. Something about their closeness warmed Melanie again and, quite suddenly, the DI decided that she'd really done enough paperwork for one late afternoon. She filed away the documents that she'd been working on in a lockable drawer and stashed the key in her suit pocket before standing from her desk.

'Anyone hungry?' Melanie asked. Edd and Chris shared a look. 'I'm pretty sure I owe you two a Chinese.'

The End

Printed in Great Britain
by Amazon

78678547R00135